Who Kidnapped the Sheriff?

Books by Larry Callen

Who Kidnapped the Sheriff?

TALES FROM TICKFAW

by LARRY CALLEN

with drawings by Stephen Gammell

The Atlantic Monthly Press · BOSTON · NEW YORK

FIRST EDITION

Library of Congress Cataloging in Publication Data

Callen, Larry.
   Who kidnapped the sheriff?

   Summary: Pat O'Leary and his friend Violet get
involved in the sheriff's kidnapping and other wild
events one summer in the town of Tickfaw.
      1. Children's stories, American.   [1. City and town
life—Fiction.   2. Humorous stories]   I. Gammell,
Stephen, ill.   II. Title.
PZ7.C134Wh   1985   [Fic]   84-72596
ISBN 0-87113-008-4

MV

Published simultaneously in Canada

PRINTED IN THE UNITED STATES OF AMERICA

To a bunch of Callens
Willa, Erin, Alex, Dashiel, Holly,
Emily, Lawrence, Dorothy, David, Ann, and Toni

And to a bunch of dear friends
whose way of life is
writing stories for children
Helen Jacob
Gloria Kamen
Marguerite Murray
Gene Namovicz
Phyllis Naylor
Peggy Thomson

Contents

Fiddle Townlee   1

Marriage License   19

Fifteen Minutes   35

The Bronze Horse   47

The Misunderstood Misunderstanding   63

The Television Caper   79

The Dog Who Wanted to Sing   95

Who Kidnapped the Sheriff?   115

The Scavenger Hunt   135

The Richest Person in Town   151

Fiddle Townlee

I don't know exactly what's wrong with Fiddle. Mom says just be nice to him, so that's what I try to do. Fiddle comes into Dad's newspaper office a couple of times a week and sits at the desk Dad assigned to him. His face is sad-looking most of the times, but he seems content enough. I've never heard Fiddle complain about anything.

"You can sit there," Dad had said, "and I'll tell you a joke or two, if I can remember any. But don't you dare put those bones in that desk drawer. You hear?"

Fiddle nodded. He picked up a chicken leg bone and held it out toward Dad to show he understood. Then he put the chicken leg bone back on top of the desk with all the other bones.

"I found me a dinosaur toe bone the other day,

Mr. O'Leary," Fiddle said, scratching around in the bones on his desk trying to find it. He picked up something and held it up for Dad to see.

"That's nice, Fiddle. Now, maybe you just better study those bones and let me get some of this work done."

I went over to take a look at whatever it was he was holding in his hand. He had shaved this morning and he was the spitting image of his brother, Mr. Vernon Townlee, who runs the bank. Fiddle only shaves about once a week, but his shirt is always clean and his shoes are always shined.

When he saw me coming over, Fiddle held something up for me to see, but before I got close enough to see if it really was a dinosaur toe bone, the front door opened and a stranger stood there. He looked at Fiddle. Then he looked at Dad. He wasn't sure who to talk to first.

"Mr. O'Leary?" he asked, looking from one to the other. He was a heavy, dark-haired man, dressed in a light-blue business suit. He had a toothy smile on his chubby face. He could have been a country preacher.

"You ever seen a genuine dinosaur toe bone?" Fiddle asked him, holding it up like an offering. It was then I got a good look at it. It was a pig knuckle.

The stranger looked at the bone. He looked at Fiddle. He wasn't certain what was happening, but the smile stayed on his face every second.

"I'm O'Leary," Dad called to him. The stranger seemed relieved. Dad stretched his hand out.

"Mr. O'Leary, you and me are going to make a fortune!"

Then the door opened again and we all turned. A thin girl with long, straight, black hair stood there, staring at us.

"It's too hot to wait outside," she said. Her chin was up and her dark eyes flicked around the room, taking us all in.

"Violet, I'm going to be talking business with this gentleman." The stranger's voice was sharp. His smile dimmed a little but never left his face.

"Pat," Dad said, "why don't you go buy the young lady a Coke while her dad and I talk business."

I looked at him, then at her. She didn't seem to be interested in going out into the heat again. But I did what he said. Fiddle stared at us as we walked toward the door.

"Hot," he said. There was the usual serious expression on his face. The girl smiled at him, but he kept staring, blank-eyed, and the smile faded from her face.

The first thing she told me was that she didn't want to be called Violet. She didn't like that name. She wanted to be called Deever. That was her last name.

The drugstore is air-conditioned. I waved to Mr. Harter. I usually sit at the shiny counter, but

5

Deever walked straight to a table, so I followed her. Mr. Harter's so old he creaks a little when he walks, but he still shuffles around and serves you at a table if you sit at one.

"You got any more money?" she asked when I had paid for the Cokes. She stuck her finger in the ice and then tasted it.

"Don't worry about it. I'll buy you another if you want."

"I mean *real* money," she said. "Like a dollar?"

The fact is I had three brand-new dollars in my pocket. I planned on spending them right in this very store for a Mother's Day present. Mom likes Mr. Harter's perfume. She calls it cologne, and it doesn't cost too much.

"Look at this," Deever said. She put three little metal cups upside down on the table.

"They call this the shell game. The cups are the shells. You didn't see me do it, but actually there's a dried pea under one of these shells. I'll bet you a nickel you can't guess which one."

But I had seen her slip the pea under the shell. It was the one on the right. I looked at her. She was grinning at me.

"Don't you have at least a nickel?" she asked.

I reached in my pocket and pulled out a nickel and slapped it on the table. I don't know if it's fair, betting when you know you are going to win. But fair or not, it sure feels good.

When I won the nickel, she gave me a hard stare,

like I had tricked her. She paid off and took a long sip of her Coke. Then her steely eyes flicked at me.

"You want to try for a dime?" she asked sharply.

She began moving the little shells around with her fingers. First one would cover the pea, then another. Then she began whipping the pea around. For a minute I lost track of it. Then I saw it again, just as she popped it under the middle shell with her pinkie. She wasn't very good at this.

After I won her dime we played for a quarter, and I won that, too. With this kind of luck I was going to buy the biggest bottle of perfume in the store.

"You got forty cents of my money," she said, her eyes even more steely. She sure was a hard loser. "You got to let me win some of it back. How about a dollar?"

I didn't like that idea at all. I don't even know why I said yes. All of a sudden one of my brand-new dollars was on the table and she was whipping the little shells around and the pea was sliding all over the place, and when she stopped moving the shells, the pea wasn't where I thought it was.

She grinned as she pulled the dollar toward her.

"Guess I got lucky that time."

I needed that dollar to buy Mom her Mother's Day present. I needed it bad.

"You want to try another dollar?" she asked, slurping the last of her Coke and not looking at me. She didn't have any table manners at all.

I had already beaten her three out of four. I would get my dollar back. Then I would quit.

The shells started moving again, faster than ever, and when she stopped I didn't have the slightest idea where that pea was. I watched my second dollar slide away.

"Got another dollar?" she asked. "I'll put up my two against your one?"

She won that dollar, too, and I was down to pocket change.

"Mother's Day is a week from Sunday," I said to her for no reason at all. I had planned so long on what I was going to buy. There wasn't time to earn another three dollars.

"One more dollar?" she nagged. Her eyes were milky-warm.

I shook my head slowly.

"Want to go home and get some more money and try to win it all back?" She made it sound like she was doing me a personal favor.

"I'm going home," I said. I slid the Coke glass away, stood up, and walked toward the door.

"Wait a minute," she called, "I'll buy you another Coke."

I was half a block away when she caught up with me. She had a Baby Ruth bar in her hand. My money had paid for it, but she didn't offer me any.

"You mad at me?" she asked.

I wasn't sure. Couldn't blame anyone but myself. We walked out of the heat into the cool of the newspaper office just in time to see my dad and her dad shake hands.

"Pat, come meet the *Tickfaw Chronicle*'s new advertising salesman," Dad said. He seemed happy about it. But that meant the two Deevers would be around for a while. I didn't know if I liked that idea at all.

When Mr. Deever and his daughter had gone, Dad told me he had arranged for them to sleep and eat at the hotel on credit.

"If that man is just half as good as he says he is, I'll be paying all my bills at the end of the month, with some left over. Maybe I'll buy that piano I always wanted," he said. He glowed as he looked at me.

"Pat, he had a good idea. We're going to run a special Mother's Day issue of the paper. He'll sell the ads to fatten up the paper, and we'll run all kinds of features on what great mothers the ladies of Tickfaw are."

"How are you going to pay a new salesman, Dad?" It wasn't really my question. It was going to be Mom's question the moment she heard what he was planning to do.

He stopped smiling and looked at me. "Well, young man, if it's any of your business, the ad campaign will pay for itself. Deever is going to take twenty percent of what he sells. We'll get eighty. He'll collect his share when he sells the ads, so I don't have to pay him a cent. Then we'll send out bills to get the rest of what we are owed at the end of the month."

It might have sounded all right to him, but he hadn't been the one who had gotten taken to the cleaners by Violet Deever. I still didn't know what I was going to do about a Mother's Day present. But I didn't say a word. Mom would do the talking for both of us.

In the morning Mr. Deever and his daughter stopped by. He got Dad to give him a letter saying he was an official employee of the *Tickfaw Chronicle*. On his way out he stopped by Fiddle's desk and looked at the bones covering the top. Fiddle had a day's growth of beard by then, and he even looked a little sleepy. He brightened up a bit when he saw Mr. Deever might be interested. Fiddle likes doing business.

"You really know a dinosaur bone from a dead cow's jaw?" Mr. Deever said.

"Course I do," Fiddle nodded solemnly. He lifted the pig-knuckle-looking bone from the desk and offered it to Mr. Deever.

Mr. Deever looked at it but his hands stayed at his sides.

"You want to buy it?" Fiddle asked, but he didn't make a sale. Fact is, he had never made a sale in his whole life. Nobody wanted to buy old chicken and pig bones.

When Mr. Deever had gone, I was left to watch over his daughter.

"I'm going home, Dad. I'll be back in a little while."

I opened the front door, but Deever was still hanging around Fiddle's desk, smiling at him, asking him questions. Next thing, she'd be pulling out her shell game.

"Come on!" I called.

Fiddle was searching around among the bones with a determined look on his face. He reached down and carefully picked one up, then offered it to her. She grinned and accepted it. That was the first time I'd ever seen him give away one of those bones.

Outside, in the heat, we walked slowly.

"That really a dinosaur toe bone?" she asked after a long silence.

"Pig knuckle," I told her.

"I like him," she said, her eyes on the heat waves rising from the sidewalk.

"Well, so do I," I said. Everybody likes Fiddle.

Mom took to Deever the moment she set eyes on her.

"Such pretty, long hair," Mom said, and Deever smiled back a warm smile.

Mom never lets me help with the baking, but she let *her* help. I just sat back and watched. I was waiting for something to happen. I didn't know what it was going to be. Maybe I expected to see Deever's eyes turn steely like they had in the drugstore. Maybe I was waiting for her to bargain Mom out of the prettiest cake they made. But the two of them just dashed around the kitchen, scattering white flour everywhere, licking sweet batter off their fingers. They baked two cakes, then smeared chocolate icing on. They paid no attention to me at all.

"We just move from town to town," Deever was saying. "Actually we never seem to settle down."

Mom nodded and began icing the second cake.

"Is it nice in Tickfaw?" Deever asked.

Mom stopped smearing icing with the knife. She straightened up and moved her shoulders around, working out the kinks.

"Why don't you stay awhile and find out?"

We didn't leave until late afternoon. Deever was as nice as could be the whole time. She walked out with a big slice of chocolate cake. And she got a hug to go with it.

Deever didn't come around the newspaper office the next day. Nor the one after that. I saw her walking near the Town Square with her father, late one afternoon when it was cooler. And one time she was leaving Harter's Drug Store when I was going in. I said hello, but she looked down and didn't answer.

I asked Dad about Mr. Deever, and he said he was doing fine. He had already sold a bunch of ads, and there was a whole day to go before deadline.

"We're going to make a mint," Dad said, smiling.

"Maybe I'll get a really nice Mother's Day present for you, Mary Dorothy." Mom was smiling at him. "And maybe a television besides," he said. Now Mom was frowning. She didn't want any television in her house.

Right about then Mr. Finley, the grocer, walked in the front door. His smile was bigger than Dad's.

"Michael O'Leary," he said, "I don't know how you managed to do it, but you've made me a happy man. If you'll sell me more ads at the same price, I'll run a whole page with you every week for the rest of the year."

Dad's smile dimmed.

"What price you talking about?"

When he heard, his smile dimmed some more.

"Why, Finley, I can't sell you a whole page of advertising for fifty dollars! It's going to cost me more than that just to set the type!"

But Mr. Finley had a contract signed and sealed by Mr. Deever, who was an official employee of the *Tickfaw Chronicle.* And Mr. Finley had already paid ten dollars to Mr. Deever.

Dad glared at the front door, then turned suddenly and kicked the desk.

"All right, all right. Mr. Deever works for me, but he isn't doing what I want him to do. At least not the money part."

Dad spent the next ten minutes on the phone and discovered three more Tickfaw merchants who had bought full-page ads for less than nothing and who had paid Mr. Deever his ten dollars. Then he called the hotel and learned that the two Deevers had checked out the night before.

"This is going to be the worst Mother's Day I ever had," Dad said.

Me, too.

I wanted to help Dad, but there was nothing I could do. I was learning fast that some people are even worse than they seem to be.

I started for home. On the way I stopped at Harter's Drug Store to buy Mom her present. But with practically nothing but pocket change, I had to settle for a bottle of honey-smelling hand lotion. Even so, Mr. Harter wrapped it nicely for me.

"I have something else for you, young fellow." He reached behind the counter and pulled out two small, brightly wrapped boxes. A card stuck out from under the yellow ribbon of one of them. *Happy Mother's Day*, it said. There was a red ribbon on the other one. *For Patrick*, it said. *Do not open until Christmas!!!* Both were signed. *V. Deever.*

I went back to the office and put my Christmas present in the bottom drawer of my desk. I was tempted to open it. I shook it one time and it rattled. I put it back and closed the drawer.

But I wasn't about to bring an unopened present from that girl to my mom. The ribbon came off easy, but Mr. Harter had used transparent tape to hold the wrapping tight.

Inside was the shell game—three shells and the pea.

What kind of gift was that? I brought it home.

"Mom, what kind of gift is this?" I hadn't even bothered to rewrap it. She smiled as she took it from me, then frowned as she read the card.

"You think you had a right to open it?" she asked.

I hadn't told her about how I lost the three dollars. And she didn't wait for an answer. She opened the box and took out the shells.

"Oh, lordy, lordy!" she said. She walked quickly to the table and put the three shells down in a straight row. She flicked the little pea around. Sometimes I could see her do it. Most times I couldn't. Then she stopped and looked straight at me. I was betting on the middle shell.

She picked up the shell on the left. It was empty. I reached over and picked up the middle shell. It was empty, too. I flipped over the right shell. Nothing. I looked at her. She was perfectly straight-faced. Then she moved her hands up waist high and turned them over, palms up. The little pea was nestled between two fingers. I was looking straight at it and I could hardly see it.

"I used to be pretty good at this when I was younger," she said. "And I must've told that child." She was smiling happily. "Pat, don't look at me in that strange way. I learned this to make money for the church bazaar."

She sat down at the table and began flicking away again. I watched her for a while and then began to get hungry.

"What's for lunch, Mom?"

"Dear, I wonder if you wouldn't mind making yourself a sandwich? Everything you need is in the refrigerator."

I went back to the *Tickfaw Chronicle* office after I had a cheese sandwich and a root beer. Fiddle was sitting at his usual desk. He was smiling for a change. His desk was totally bare. All of the bones were gone. I'd never seen him sitting behind a bare desk before.

"Where are the bones, Fiddle?"

He sat up straight and proud. He had shaved this morning, and the week was only halfway through.

"I sold them," he said. "I sold the dinosaur toe bone and I sold the rest of them, too. It was like business."

He sat there, smiling happily. He doesn't smile that often. His hand moved like a piano player across the desk, touching where the bones had been. Then he leaned over and opened the desk drawer, and I waited for him to pull out all those dry bones he claimed he had sold. But that's not what happened.

His hand came out of the drawer holding a brand-new dollar bill. He laid it flat on the desk, then reached in the drawer again. Out came a second brand-new dollar bill. He placed it next to the first. He smiled up at me. His hand went back into the drawer one more time. Out came a third new bill.

My brand-new Mother's Day dollar bills were staring up at me! Deever was the one who had bought those bones. She knew it would make Fiddle happy.

I went over and sat at my desk. I slid open the bottom drawer and looked at her brightly wrapped Christmas package. I rattled it. It was just the right size for a dinosaur toe bone.

I looked over at Fiddle, sitting at his desk, gently touching each of the three brand-new dollars he had earned all by himself.

I looked back at my Christmas present. Wasn't any doubt in my mind what was inside. Maybe I'd leave it right where it was. Christmas wasn't that far off. By then Fiddle might feel like smiling again.

I wonder if Violet Deever had thought about that, too?

Marriage License

The crate of oranges just sat there on the steps of St. Agnes' Church. I didn't know then all the trouble they were going to cause.

Jenna Jones and I had been invited to be a part of the wedding party of Mr. Henry Harter and Miss Nola Mae Miller. It was a special honor because they were our good friends. Besides, it was the first time in the history of the town of Tickfaw that an eighty-year-old man would be marrying an eighty-year-old woman.

"Something old, something new," Mr. Harter had said when he invited us. I figured out later that they were the old and we were the new.

St. Agnes' was about a quarter filled when we got

inside for the wedding rehearsal. Mom smiled and waved to Jenna and me. Mr. Harter and Miss Nola Mae were in the front pew talking to Father Tom Fulsome. I watched until the priest walked way. Then I asked about the oranges.

"What oranges?" asked Miss Nola Mae Miller.

"Oh, my dear," said Mr. Henry Harter, "it was supposed to be a surprise for you when you left the church. I bought a crate from Finley's Grocery especially for you."

"Terrible waste of money," she said.

"But they're full of vitamin C and good for colds. I heard you say you adored them!"

"You heard wrong, Henry, as usual. I haven't eaten an orange in sixty years. I like the color. I don't like the fruit."

He glared at her. She glared back. They had found something new to quarrel about.

When Father Tom Fulsome called to them, they were still glaring.

"Time to start the rehearsal," he said.

Miss Nola Mae turned on him. "My feet are too tired right now, Father."

"I feel pretty much the same," said Mr. Harter.

Father Tom smiled and nodded. "Well, perhaps it's just as well. You two sit right there, and we'll put on a wedding for you. Maybe you can learn just as much from seeing as from doing." He began looking around the church, searching for something. Then his eyes settled on me.

"Pat, come up here a minute. Jenna, you too."

I wasn't exactly sure what was on his mind, but I got up and walked to where he was standing. Jenna sat right where she was.

"Come on up, Jenna. You two can substitute for the bride and groom."

She slowly walked over to us. She didn't want to come up front with all those people watching. Some of them were kids. We were both going to take a razzing when this was over.

"Now," said Father Tom, "pretend you have just walked up the aisle. You're standing here in front of me." He turned to the old couple. "You two watch what's happening up here and stop glaring at one another."

He began reading the wedding ceremony, and I began feeling even dumber than before. People were smirking. I wondered what Jenna was thinking.

We stood there, close together, listening, looking at the book in the priest's hands. I shifted the weight on my feet, and our shoulders touched. Jenna's head slowly turned. Our eyes met only for a second. We both knew it was pretend. But that didn't stop the feeling that something special was happening.

"Now," said Father Tom. His eyes lifted from the book. He looked down at us and grinned. "If anyone in Tickfaw knows reason why these two should not be married, speak now . . ."

I found myself wishing that nobody would say a word.

"I do!" shouted a voice from the back of the church.

I turned around quick. I recognized that voice. Standing there, right in the middle of the aisle, was Violet Deever, her smile full of mischief. I hadn't seen her since her father left town, only one step ahead of the Sheriff.

Now she was back. It was the start of more trouble. I knew it.

She came prancing up the aisle. Then Mom called softly to her, and Deever walked over and gave her a hug. The two of them sat together and talked softly.

"All right," said Father Tom, "let's get back to work here." He turned to the old couple. "Have you two been watching? You want to come on up here now, and we'll run through the ceremony one more time?"

"Not ready yet," said Mr. Harter, twitching on the pew.

"Me neither," said Miss Nola Mae.

Father Tom shook his head. "Henry, I'll buy those oranges from you if it'll settle things. Meanwhile, Pat and Jenna, let's give it one more try."

But Jenna wasn't there anymore. I looked around and she had returned to her seat.

"Jenna?" asked Father Tom. She just shook her

head. She'd had enough of getting married for one day.

"What a day!" the priest said, closing his book.

"I'll do it!" shouted Deever and came running up before anyone could stop her.

I glared at her. A pretend marriage to Jenna was one thing. But if Father Tom thought I was going to pretend getting married to Deever, he could just go say his prayers. I stared at him. He smiled and shrugged his shoulders. It didn't make any difference to him who I got married to. I looked over at Jenna. She was doing her own glaring at Deever. I truly hoped Jenna was sorry for having gotten me in this predicament.

Deever stood right next to me and snuggled in close. I pulled away, but she just grinned and moved close again.

Father Tom started the ceremony all over again. He said the words. I played like I gave her the ring. Nobody said a word this time when he asked if anybody objected.

"What God has joined, men must not divide. Amen." He smiled at us, then looked over our heads at Mr. Harter and Miss Nola Mae. "At this point I would pronounce you husband and wife," he said.

He closed his book and walked toward the old couple. Deever had turned to face me.

"You can kiss me if you want to, Patrick O'Leary," she whispered.

I spun away toward where Jenna was sitting. Her face was squinched like she was mad. That was enough of weddings for one day. I walked fast down the aisle and out of the church.

I was all the way to the school yard before I slowed down. There wasn't anybody on the basketball court, so I kept on walking. I stayed away from home until I got hungry. Mom was making cold chicken sandwiches for my brother, E.J., when I walked in. When she saw me she took out more bread.

"How's it feel to be a married man, Pat?" asked E.J.

I ignored him. He's older, but he's dumber.

"You missed the good part at the church, Pat," Mom said, spreading mayonnaise on bread. "Henry and Nola Mae made up after you left and they went through their own rehearsal. It was a beautiful thing to watch. Then, after it was over, Father Tom asked Henry for the marriage license, and he said Nola Mae had it, and she said he had it, and they started fussing all over again."

"They sure seem to fuss a lot," said E.J. He was half finished with his sandwich.

"Those two are set in their ways," said Mom. "But they'll find some rules to go by." She put another sandwich in front of E.J. and looked at me. "Eat your sandwich, Pat."

But I didn't want to eat. I wanted to talk to Jenna.

I called, but nobody answered. The weather was so hot, she might be outside and not able to hear the phone. I decided to walk over, and I had made it as far as the Town Square when I saw Deever sitting on a bench. And worse still, she saw me.

"Come sit by me, Pat," she called. She moved aside a can of cola and a bag of potato chips to make room. But I didn't want to sit down.

"Won't hurt you to sit down," she said. "What are you going to do about what happened at the church?"

"What do you mean, what am I going to do?"

She picked up the potato chips and offered them to me.

"Actually, Patrick O'Leary, you married me. We are husband and wife. What are you going to do about that?"

It was the dumbest thing I ever heard. I looked at her to see if she was serious. There wasn't even a piece of a smile on her face. She sat there, head tilted, staring.

"I'm waiting for an answer, Patrick O'Leary!"

"An answer to what?"

"Where are we going to live? Will your father buy the groceries? Mine sure won't. He'll be pleased you took me off his hands."

She kept babbling on.

"Deever, go kiss a toad!" I had only stopped to be polite. It was Jenna I wanted to talk to. "We were just practicing. People don't get married

27

when they don't even know they are getting married."

She stood up suddenly, hands on hips. "You answer me this, Pat. Was that a real priest up there saying those words?"

"Well . . ."

"And did he say all the right words?"

"I don't know . . ."

"You heard him say 'I now pronounce you husband and wife'?"

"I didn't hear him say that!"

"You know you did, Pat. And even if you didn't, that doesn't mean he didn't say it. I heard him say it. Everybody heard him say it. Actually, I'm surprised you didn't hear him say it, because he really did say it."

"It doesn't make any difference what he said, Deever. I didn't know I was getting married. I thought it was a rehearsal. That can't be a real marriage."

"Well, it was!"

"Well, it wasn't!" I turned and walked away.

"Patrick O'Leary! Do I come live at your house or what?" Deever's voice trailed after me.

Jenna wasn't home. Maybe for the best. I was so angry I was spitting nails. I took the long way back to my house. When I got there, Ezmerelda and her two new puppies were sound asleep on the front porch. I tiptoed past them, but Ez opened one eye to see who it was.

Mom was sitting in the front room, reading a book about mind reading. She looked up at me and smiled. She didn't say anything. It was like she was trying to send me a message without talking. Dad was in his overstuffed chair with a book in his lap, too. It was quiet.

"Violet stopped by, Pat," said Mom. "She said she was going for her things and would be back. What did she mean by that?"

I told them both what Deever had said about us being married. Dad stopped reading.

"Ridiculous!" he said.

"That's what I told her. Dumb. But she's got it set in her head."

"Now, dears, both of you," said Mom, "there's more going on here than meets the eye. That child is looking for a permanent home, and it looks like she has decided on us. I don't know that I like the idea, and I don't know that I don't. But I do know that for us to kick her out when she returns won't solve the real problem."

I went to bed not long after that. It took me a good while to go to sleep. I kept wondering if Deever really was going to come back and try to move in. I didn't know what I would do if she did.

It was practically midnight when I finally decided I could relax and go to sleep. I settled into my pillow. I hadn't been asleep two minutes when E.J. came home from his date. First he stomped around in his room. That woke me up. Then he came into my room to make sure he had done a good job.

"Pat?"

"What?"

"Why is that girl sleeping on the front porch?"

He was talking about Deever. He had to be. I sat up and tried to shake the sleep out of my head.

"I asked her but she wouldn't say a word," E.J. went on. "I told her she could come in and sleep on the sofa if she didn't have anyplace else to go, and she still wouldn't say a word."

I stood up and wobbled out of the room. I had a little trouble getting the front door open in the dark. When I finally got outside, there wasn't anybody sleeping on the porch. Maybe she was out there, watching. Or maybe she had gone off someplace. I felt sorry for her, with bugs and mosquitoes and stuff like that filling up the dark. I went back to bed and tried to get to sleep, but I was a long time doing it.

I'd probably never see her again. That didn't bother me one bit. But she wasn't a dishonest person like her father. I had seen enough of her to know that. She was just pushy. That was her problem.

Suddenly Mom was shaking my shoulder. The smell of breakfast bacon filled the room. But I was in the middle of a dream.

In my dream Deever was standing there, wearing

a white dress I had seen Mom wear a hundred times.

"And I will need a brand-new wardrobe," she was saying. "And I will want all new furniture for the front room. And I must have a new stove and refrigerator. And that's just the things I want by tomorrow morning."

"I don't want to be married, Deever," I was saying when Mom shook me even harder. When I opened my eyes, Mom was smiling. I don't know if she heard my dream or not. I don't think I said anything aloud, but you never know about dreams.

After breakfast I sat out on the front porch, just wondering about things. And that's when I found it, tucked in a corner of the porch, right about where Deever must have slept the night before. It was an envelope with my name written lightly on the outside. Just *Patrick*. Nothing else. I opened it.

It was the marriage license that had been lost at the church. It was signed and dated by Father Tom. But in the blank spaces where Mr. Harter's and Miss Nola Mae's names should have been, there were other names.

". . . joined in the bonds of matrimony," it said, "are Patrick Wilson O'Leary and Violet Gertrude Deever. . . ."

I had it in my shirt pocket that afternoon on the way to Jenna's house. She was fixing chicken on the barbecue grill and she didn't look mad anymore.

When I asked if I could help her, Jenna smiled at me, and the marriage license was suddenly heavy in my pocket. I could feel it through the cloth of my shirt.

Should I keep it? Maybe someday I would meet Deever again when both of us were grown up, and Jenna and I were married and had a bunch of kids, and Deever was married to somebody else and had an even bigger bunch of kids. I would show her the license and we would laugh and remember things and say how much fun it had been way back then.

But that would never happen. I would probably never see her again. It bothered me, sitting there with Jenna and having that piece of paper in my pocket. It seemed like as long as I kept it, Deever and I *were* married.

"Pat, the fire's going down. Could you fix it?" asked Jenna.

I put half a dozen sticks on the dying fire, but they wouldn't catch. I reached into my pocket and took out the license. I laid it gently on the coals and put the smallest of the twigs on top.

"What did you put in the fire, Pat?"

"Just a piece of paper with some words on it," I answered, as the hot coals touched the paper and little flames grew.

We sat in silence and watched the fire until Jenna's mother called.

"Pat, it's your mother on the phone."

But it wasn't my mother who wanted to talk to me.

"Pat, Violet's here. She says her father's in New Orleans but she doesn't know anyone there. She likes Tickfaw better. I told her she could stay with us for a while. She wants to talk to you." Then Deever's voice.

"Pat? When are you coming home?"

"I'm busy."

"Your mom says I can stay at your house and I called my father and he says OK. And you know what else?"

I wasn't one bit interested, but she told me anyway.

"Mr. Harter has given me a part-time job at the drugstore. Isn't that nice?"

I hung onto the phone and let her talk. Jenna had followed me in and was standing in the doorway, watching and listening.

"Pat," said Deever, "do you know what I'm doing this very minute?"

"Uh, no."

"I'm helping your mom cook your very favorite supper. Red beans and rice. I want you sitting at the table at six sharp."

"Deever, I don't have to listen to you. You're not my mother."

"Of course not, Patrick. We are husband and wife. And don't you be one single minute late, you hear?"

She was starting that again. I'd had more than enough. I was ready to slam the phone down when I heard her say to Mom:

"That ought to get him hopping."

Fifteen Minutes

You've got fifteen minutes to make up your mind," Mom said. She put the red toothbrush and the green toothbrush on the table, side by side. "If you haven't decided by the time Violet gets here, I'll do the deciding."

My old toothbrush had been yellow, and its bristles were soft and bent. These two looked pretty good. Maybe the red would be best. I sat down at the table and studied them.

Two minutes later Violet Deever walked in, big smile on her face like she owned the world.

"What're you doing?" she asked.

"Nothing."

She saw the toothbrushes on the table. She reached for one, but I pushed her hand away.

"Pat, stop that," she said. "I asked your mother to buy me a toothbrush. One of those is mine."

Mom heard her and shouted from the kitchen that I had asked first so I had first choice.

"Twelve minutes left to decide, Pat."

"Oh," said Deever. She sat down on the other side of the table and studied the toothbrushes.

"They're both nice, aren't they?" she asked. "You know which one you're going to take yet?"

"Whichever one I want," I said. I wasn't going to have her trying to make me take the one *she* didn't want.

"Maybe you ought to take the red one," she said, touching the end of the red handle. "It's very nice. The bristles look very straight."

Then a sly look crossed her face and I knew she was playing one of her games again. She was going to try and trick me. Well, this time I wasn't going to be tricked. This time I would do the tricking.

"Deever, don't touch them. Mom said I had first choice, and that means first touching, too."

I looked closely at the green one. If she wanted me to take the red one, she must've seen something special about the green one. Or maybe she just liked the color best.

The green one looked a little bit longer than the red one. But maybe it was just where I was sitting. I moved them closer together to compare size.

"It doesn't seem right that you can touch them and I can't," she said. "One of them is going to be mine, isn't it? Well, I don't want you touching my toothbrush. A toothbrush is a very personal thing, Pat. People don't go around touching other people's toothbrushes."

All her talk was getting in the way of my deciding which one I wanted.

"Mom, make Violet stop talking. I can't think when she is talking."

Deever looked at her wristwatch. "You've got only ten more minutes to decide, Pat."

Now she was really trying to get me confused.

"Mom, do I really have only ten more minutes?"

But Mom didn't answer, and Deever smiled and pointed to her watch. Then she drew a little circle around the red toothbrush with her finger. She didn't say a word, but she might as well have.

I looked at the toothbrushes and then I looked at her. She kept telling me the red one was best. She wanted me to think she wanted the green one. But suppose it was one of her tricks? Maybe it was the red one she wanted. Well, two could play at that game.

"I haven't really decided yet, but I think that I might just take the green one," I said.

The expression on her face didn't change a whit. Not an eyelid flickered. She stared me in the eye, daring me to guess what she was thinking.

"You have nine minutes left, Pat," she said.

But I wasn't going to be rushed into anything. I stood up and went to the kitchen for a glass of water. Mom was slicing tomatoes and cucumbers and celery for a salad.

"Mom, do I *have* to decide in fifteen minutes?"

"Decide about what, dear?"

"Aw, Mom. You know. The toothbrush. Violet is sitting right there, trying to get me to take the one she doesn't want."

Now Mom was washing lettuce at the sink.

"I can't see what difference the color of a toothbrush makes, Pat. Just pick one and be done with it."

But she didn't understand. I went back into the dining room. And I saw right away that Deever had moved both brushes. The green one had been closest to where I was sitting. Now the red one was closest.

"A fly lit on it," she said.

"What?"

"I wouldn't take the green one if I were you, Pat. While you were gone a fly lit on it. Maybe it laid some eggs. How would you like brushing your teeth with a bunch of fly eggs?"

"I'm not listening to that kind of stuff, Deever. I'm picking the one I want. Not the one you *don't* want."

"Know what color fly eggs are, Pat?"

I was looking at the toothbrushes. The bristles of both were snowy white. It looked like there might be a fleck of something on the bristles of the green one, but it surely wasn't fly eggs. Maybe dust is all.

"They are green. That's what color fly eggs are."

I flicked the bristles of the green toothbrush with my finger and whatever was on them disappeared. But if I took the green one, I would wash it with scalding water anyway.

The screen door slammed in the kitchen and I could hear my brother, E.J., asking Mom if he had time to take a shower before dinner. Then he rushed into the dining room. When he saw us, he slowed.

"What are you two doing?" he asked.

"Pat is selecting a toothbrush," said Deever. "He has been at it for exactly seven minutes so far."

E.J. wasn't interested in what we were doing. He kept on walking. A minute later he came back into the room, holding his own toothbrush.

"Mom," he called, "I think I need a toothbrush worse than anybody. Could I have one of those on the table?"

"I get one," I told him. "Mom says Violet gets the other."

"But if you *could* have one, E.J., which one would you take?" asked Deever.

He stopped at the table and stared down at the two brushes.

"That all the colors there are? Mine is orange. I'd like another orange one."

"Don't you think Pat ought to take the red one?" asked Deever.

E.J. didn't answer. When he had gotten a promise out of Mom to buy him an orange toothbrush, he headed back to the shower.

"I think he secretly wants the red brush, Patrick," said Deever. "But you have first choice."

I'd already wasted more than half of my time and I still didn't know which one I wanted. I like red. It's a bright, kind of loud color. I wouldn't want red clothes, except maybe a tie. Dad's got a red sport coat that he wore one time only, and then swore he would never wear again because everybody kept making jokes about it. But a toothbrush is different. I never heard a toothbrush joke in my whole life.

"Pat, have you ever broken a tooth?" asked Deever.

I was just getting started on my thinking and she got me distracted again.

Mom's not going to fool around. At the end of the fifteen minutes, she's going to decide who gets what color.

"The reason I asked, Pat, is that when you break a tooth, it means a friend will die. I had that happen to me when I was only six years old. It wasn't exactly a person-friend. It was a hamster. But it broke my heart. You know what my hamster's name was, Pat?"

"Deever, will you please let me think?"

She says I ought to take the red one. She knows I'm not going to take the one she wants me to. That means she knows I'll take the green one. And that means she wants the red one. If she just keeps quiet a little bit longer, I'll have this thing puzzled out.

"Red is a very lucky color, Pat. Did you know it can even help you if you have a poor memory? All you have to do is tie a red string around a finger on your left hand—"

"And remember why you tied it there," I snarled. She just wouldn't shut up.

"Mom, what time is it?"

"You have five minutes left, Pat," said Deever. "You are surely taking a long time to make up your mind."

She got up and went into the kitchen. I could hear low voices and laughter. Then she came back, crunching on a celery stick.

She says I should take the red one. But she also knows I won't do it, because she is telling me to do it. But if I'm smart enough to figure that out, then I'll take the red one, and she'll be left with the green one.

Suppose she's figured out that I'll figure it out. Which one does she really want, then?

I was getting confused.

I looked at her. She was still chewing on the celery. Was she trying to say something to me with that green stick? She smiled at me, still chewing.

Maybe I ought to get back to thinking about which one I want, instead of which one she wants. The green one is pretty. Kind of a grass green. I've got to get that business about fly eggs out of my mind. That's just trickery.

43

Lots of nice-looking things are green. Lawns are green. Leaves are green. Olives. Emeralds. Watermelons.

Watermelons.

But the sweet part on the inside is red.

"Do you know anything about rotten garbage, Pat? It's ugly and slimy and probably full of fly eggs. Did I ever tell you that once I had a possum for a pet? Possums eat garbage. Did you know that? And they have funny green stuff growing all over their teeth."

I used to like brushing my teeth. Made them feel clean. And I like the taste of toothpaste. They put something in it that tickles your tongue. Sometimes when we run out of toothpaste, I brush with salt, and I even like the taste of that. But I wasn't looking forward to brushing my teeth ever again.

"What time do you think it is, Pat?" she asked.

"All right, Deever. Which one do you *really* want?"

"Oh, I don't have a real preference. I just thought the red one would be nice for you."

I balled my fist. I knew she wasn't going to tell me the truth.

"You're just saying that, right? I'll take the red one, and then you will get the green one, which is the one you really want. I know what you're trying to do, Deever."

She tilted her head, lifted her eyebrows, and kind

of sniffed, like she was saying I had a right to my opinion even if I was wrong.

"Ma!" called E.J. from the bathroom. "There's a big green fly in here."

"See there!" said Deever. "I told you so."

Mom came to the rescue with a flyswatter clutched in her hand. I heard a single *whack!,* and she came walking out with a grin of victory on her face.

"Two minutes to go, Pat," she said as she passed.

"Mom, it's not fair to put all this pressure on me. I haven't had a single minute to think. Deever's been here jabbering away the whole time."

"I'll be back in two minutes," Mom said.

I whirled on Deever. I wanted to yell at her to go away, but she wasn't smiling like she was winning the war or anything. There was a kind of hurt look on her face.

"I thought I had been helping you, Pat," she said.

"Deever, a guy doesn't need help to pick the right color for a toothbrush."

"All right, then. I won't say another word." She sat back in her chair and looked at me. The hurt look stayed on her face. Now she was trying to make me feel guilty.

"One minute!" called Mom.

Which one? Red one? Green one? Ruby one? Emerald one? Somehow I knew she wanted the red one. I just knew it.

45

I could hear Mom stirring around in the kitchen. She was going to come marching out here any second.

"All right. I've decided," I said.

I stretched my hand out over the toothbrushes. I paused over the red one and looked at Deever's face, but I couldn't tell a thing. Then I moved my hand over the green one. Still nothing.

I scooped my hand down and grabbed the green one, watching her from the corner of my eye. Her face lit up like a Christmas tree.

"Good!" she said.

Now I knew. I dropped the green toothbrush and grabbed the red one. I pulled it close to me. This time I had won.

"Time's up!" yelled Mom.

I grinned at Deever and waited for her smile to fade. But it didn't happen.

She reached out in her dainty way. With two fingers she plucked the green toothbrush from the table.

"Wonderful!" she said. "Green is my favorite color."

The
Bronze Horse

He died on Saturday afternoon.

On Saturday morning, Violet Deever and I played cards with Mr. Beauregard Miller on the wooden bench in the Town Square. Deever had never played before. But Mr. Beauregard Miller and I had, lots of times. We always sat on the same bench. It was the one right in the middle of the square, next to the bronze horse. And we always played fan-tan.

"I like this spot," he said more than once. "I'd like to stay here forever. In the middle of summer it's the only cool spot in town. I told the Mayor once I wanted to be buried here, but he didn't much like the idea of turning the Town Square into a graveyard."

Mr. Beauregard Miller was a short, bent man. They say a long time ago he had been a bigger man. He was even a soldier. We heard a new war story almost every week. Sometimes we heard the same one over again, changed a bit.

Deever was listening to his story, eyes sparkling and mouth kind of hanging open. Suddenly she cupped a smile behind her hand and leaned over toward me.

"He cheated," she whispered.

I already knew it. Sometimes I would see him cheat and sometimes I wouldn't. But I never said anything, because when we finished playing, he would scrape all the pennies he had won into his gnarled hand and plop them down in front of somebody else. Then he would give us a big smile from under his bushy mustache.

"I like playing fan-tan," he would say. "But I like winning better."

Saturday afternoon, when Deever and I passed by the square again, he was alone. He saw me and waved, and that's when it happened.

"Pat, I got a problem," he said. He held both his hands to his chest. His teeth crunched. He was having trouble with his breathing.

"Reach into my coat pocket," he whispered.

I stared at him. I was scared. He wasn't acting normal at all. But he was my friend. I did what he said and pulled out a thin envelope.

He looked kindly at me. "You might want to read

it at my funeral," he said softly. He almost smiled. His mouth opened to say something more, but what came out was only a sound.

"Haaaaaaaa." It was a sandpaper kind of sound.

Mr. Beauregard Miller died on that bench, and Violet Deever and I were there, standing close, watching when he did it.

I ran. It was all I could think to do.

"Dad! Mr. Beauregard Miller is dead!"

After that, the real problems started.

I was in the *Tickfaw Chronicle* office about a week later, helping Dad address newspapers to mail subscribers, when Emil Broussard rushed through the front door. He went right to Dad's desk and stood there, shifting his skinny frame from one foot to another.

"I got a political advertisement I want to run in your paper," he said. "Town Council election's not too far off."

"Why, Emil," Dad said, "you only just got out of college."

Emil smiled and shifted his feet some more and started talking about being ambitious and wanting to help people. The calendar on the wall behind Dad was hanging crooked, and Emil straightened it. Then he picked up a pencil Dad had dropped on the floor a day or so before.

"Governor is what I want to be," he said, sticking his hands in his pockets. "Papa says I will be a good one. But it's hard as heck to wait."

He finally handed Dad the advertisement.

"Oh, and something else, Mr. O'Leary. I got a pretty good story for you." He put his hands back in his pockets. "You still got time for the next issue of the paper?"

Dad stared at him. He didn't much like Emil. I heard him say once you need a real good reason to like a lawyer.

"Maybe," Dad said.

I learned a lot of things in the next few minutes. My friend, Mr. Beauregard Miller, had been one of the founding fathers of Tickfaw. He never told me that. He had been a rich farmer way back then, and he had donated to Tickfaw the whole piece of land that makes up the Town Square.

"And you know who paid for the bronze horse that sits in the center of the square?" Emil asked.

Mr. Beauregard Miller had told us horse stories a couple of times. I hadn't known if they were true when he told them. Most of them were about how in World War I he rode a big bay horse across green fields in France. The poor horse got shot. He said more than once he was going back there someday and go horseback riding when nobody was shooting at him.

"Mr. O'Leary, you're not going to believe this story," said Emil. He sat down next to Dad's desk and lowered his voice. "I sneaked a look at Beauregard's will. It says the town can keep the square, but he still owns the bronze horse. He wants it to be set on top of his grave."

The young lawyer's voice was getting loud. "Now, you know, Mr. O'Leary, something's wrong here. That bronze horse has been in the square for sixty years. I played on that horse when I was a kid and my father probably did the same. Beauregard can't take back that horse. I got kids on the way, too, probably, you know."

Now that was a scary thought. No kid who was forewarned would likely want to say "Daddy" to Emil Broussard.

"He can't make us move that horse to the grave-yard!" he whined. "That man always played hard to win, but we can't let him win this time. I'm going to the courthouse and check the records. Got to be something we can do to keep that bronze horse right where it is." He moved toward the door. Then he stopped suddenly and turned.

"Oh, and Mr. O'Leary, I've decided to donate my legal services to the town in this matter. If you use my name in your newspaper story, I'd appreciate it. And maybe you want to say something about the election."

Emil wasn't out of the door five minutes when it slammed open. Miss Nola Mae Miller stood there, leaning on a walking stick. She was Mr. Beauregard Miller's sister, and even older than him.

"First of all," she yelled, "I don't want any horse

stuck on top of a grave I am going to be buried in someday." She stopped yelling a minute and rubbed her bad ear.

"What's that?" she asked. She stared at my father. "Don't you say anything disrespectful to me, young man!"

The thing about Dad is that he knows when to talk and when not to say a word. Every single argument he has won from me was when he was staring hard rather than talking.

"You young people don't understand anything at all about dying," she went on.

"Miss Nola Mae," Dad said, taking her arm and moving her toward the door, "I promise I will do what I can."

When she was gone, Dad turned and looked in my direction.

"She just doesn't like horses, Pat." Then he told me a story I hadn't heard before.

"Sixty years ago . . ." he paused. ". . . Imagine that. . . . Sixty years ago Beauregard Miller bought himself a fine horse. Nola Mae wanted to ride it, and at first he said no and then he said yes. The horse was spirited and let her sit in the saddle for a while, then tossed her on her bottom. She didn't break anything but her pride.

"Then Beauregard went off to war. When he came back, the farm was going fine, so he used some of the money to buy land that's now the Town Square. Then he went to New Orleans and had them make him a bronze horse exactly like the one that was killed under him in France.

"The day they put the bronze horse in the Town Square, Nola Mae walked by and smacked the horse with a stick. She's done exactly the same thing almost every day for sixty years. If that horse wasn't made of bronze, it would've been beaten to death by now."

The front door opened softly, and we turned. It was Mr. Vernon Townlee, the banker and my friend Fiddle's brother. He stood tall and thin in the doorway. A black bow tie separated his head from the rest of him. He didn't say a word until he was sure he had our full attention.

"Mr. O'Leary, I'd get a reporter and a photographer over to the Town Square right this minute, if I were you." He spoke softly like he always did, but there was an urgency to his voice.

"Pat, grab one of the cameras," Dad called to me, but he said that mainly for Mr. Townlee's benefit, because we only have one camera.

The crowd at the square was pretty big for the middle of the day. Then I saw what had brought them together. A ring of kids surrounded the bronze horse. They had their backs to it and were holding hands. The crowd clapped and cheered them on. Before we even got close, I saw who the ringleader was.

Violet Deever had found another way to get into trouble. She had no business doing this. She hadn't really known Mr. Beauregard Miller. She didn't know that he had been a friend to nearly every kid in town, or that he wanted that horse for his grave. She was just stirring things up, like always.

"What's happening, Violet?" called Dad, sliding a film plate into the camera.

She broke off hand-holding with the kids next to her.

"Mr. O'Leary, these kids say somebody is trying to move the horse and they don't know why and they don't want it moved."

I went up to her. "Deever, we got to talk."

"Some other time, Pat. I'm busy right now."

"That's what we got to talk about," I said, but she had already rejoined the circle of kids.

Dad took several pictures. I went around the ring and got the names of all the boys and girls. I passed Deever up without a word, but she wasn't paying any attention to me, either.

"Are you planning to put our pictures in the *Tickfaw Chronicle*, Mr. O'Leary?" she asked. Dad smiled and said he was.

"Good. Then we will stay right here and fight to the end."

Dad and I edged our way out of the crowd, but Deever's voice called me back.

"Pat, we've been out here a long time. Would you please ask your mother or somebody if I could have a tuna-fish sandwich?"

Deever never got her tuna-fish sandwich. By

suppertime the rebellion had ended, because all of
the parents had collected their kids. But that didn't
end everything — not at all. The story and the pictures ran in Thursday's paper, and the Mayor called
a meeting that night after supper.

While we were walking to the meeting I told
Deever about Mr. Beauregard Miller wanting to be
buried under the horse.

"Why did you wait so long to tell me, Pat?"

"You dimwit! I tried to tell you a bunch of times
and you wouldn't listen."

"Then, Patrick, you should have tried harder."

When we got to the Town Hall, Deever and I sat
in the front row with some of the other kids.

"The thing is," the Mayor said, "we don't want
to move that horse, but maybe we've got to. We
don't own it. Dead or alive, Beauregard owns it.
And if he wants it on his grave, he's got a legal right
to it."

"Mr. Mayor," a voice yelled from the back of the
hall. It was Miss Nola Mae Miller, standing straight
with the help of her cane. "I don't want it on *my*
grave!"

"Nola Mae," said the Mayor, "I wish I could help
you, because I'm on your side. The whole town of
Tickfaw is on your side."

"Not anymore!" yelled Deever. "Let's have a
vote!"

"What's that?" The Mayor looked in the direction the voice had come from. When he saw it

was Deever, he smiled and turned back to the crowd.

"Now," he said, "somebody's got to move that horse, and Claiborne Broussard here is the only one in town with a truck big enough to do it, so I asked him to check it out."

Mr. Claiborne Broussard stood up and put his hands on his hips. He's a big man, especially around the middle. He's the one who has the contract to repair all the parish and state roads around Tickfaw. Folks say it's no coincidence our state governor's named Broussard, too.

"I been studying on it," he said, putting his weight on one large leg, then shifting to the other. You could see he wasn't comfortable talking with all these people looking at him. "I'm guessing that old horse weighs close to a ton. We got trucks big enough to carry it, but we got nothing that'll lift it into the truck. And I don't think you'll find anything closer than New Orleans. Cost a fortune to get a piece of heavy-lift equipment from there to here." He sat down and looked relieved his speech was over.

That's when his son, Emil, the lawyer, held up his hand.

"I've been checking on the legal part, like you told me to, Papa. And I want all you folks to know I'm offering this legal help to the town absolutely free, as my patriotic duty." He hunched his shoulders back and pulled at his thin, red tie and smiled

58

around at all the people. Then he turned to the Mayor.

"I think I know how to solve this problem. I have a very good plan, but it needs some working on."

"How long will your plan take, Emil?" the Mayor asked. "According to Fred Fulkerson at the funeral parlor, we got to do something quick."

"We can have Beauregard buried by tomorrow morning," Emil said, smiling broadly. He turned to face his audience as if he were ready to take a bow. His eyes twinkled as he unfolded his plan.

"What does his will say? It says that he wants to be buried *under* the bronze horse. But we don't have to move the horse one inch to do that. You see what I'm getting at?"

Even I did.

"But I ain't keen on turning the Town Square into any graveyard," said the Mayor.

"One grave ain't no cemetery," said a voice from the back.

"He always beat the pants off me at fan-tan," said another voice. "I suspicioned he might be doing something sneaky with the cards. Now the old codger is trying to steal our bronze horse."

I didn't understand this kind of talk. Mr. Beauregard Miller had been a friend of everybody in this room when he was living. And he hadn't even asked for anything except what was his.

"All we got to do is dig a hole in the ground alongside the bronze horse," said Emil.

59

Deever suddenly leaned close to me.

"Pat, didn't you tell me his will said he wanted to be buried *under* the bronze horse?"

She was talking to me, but loud enough for everyone in the room to hear.

Mr. Claiborne Broussard stood up again. "You start digging under that horse, you're going to have a cave-in, for sure."

So the grown-ups put their heads together again and decided, instead of having the grave running alongside of the horse, they would have it at right angles. They would dig the hole so that when the coffin was finally lowered into the ground, at least Mr. Beauregard Miller's feet would be under the horse.

I looked over at Deever. She was looking straight at me. She knew we had kind of won. I smiled at her. It might even have been the first time I ever smiled at her.

But when I thought about it later, it still didn't seem right. That man had done too much for the town. He'd been a good friend to me and the rest of the kids. If his will said he wanted the horse moved, they ought to have found a way to move the horse.

They threw dirt on top of his casket and put up a nice marble marker saying he was the town founder and that's why he was being buried in the Town Square, almost like they were apologizing. Then they began saying prayers over him.

I wanted to do something. But what?

Then Deever nudged me. "Pat, you still got Mr. Beauregard Miller's letter stuffed in your pocket?"

I had forgotten the letter. I checked in my pocket and there it was. I smoothed it out, and we read it while everyone prayed. This time both of us were smiling. I eased over to Dad and let him read it. When the praying was finished and it was still quiet, Dad walked over and stood beside Father Tom Fulsome and held up his hand.

"I've just been given a letter from Mr. Beauregard Miller addressed to all of us in Tickfaw. Kind of like he is speaking to us from the grave." Every eye in the Town Square moved from Dad to the mound of dirt on top of the grave.

"I'll read it to you," he said, "and then, if it's all right with Father Tom, we can all go home."

Dad held the letter out in front of him and adjusted his glasses on his nose.

"To all you fine people in Tickfaw," he read. "I want to thank you for burying me in the Town Square. It's my very favorite spot, and it's where I wanted to be buried in the first place.

"I knew you couldn't move that dang horse."

The
Misunderstood
Misunderstanding

Why is everybody sulking?" I whispered to Jenna. "I thought we were supposed to be having fun."

It was a backyard party Mr. Harter was giving for Miss Nola Mae, and everybody had been having a great time until a few minutes ago. All of a sudden it was like a storm, only without the rain. You couldn't see the lightning, but you could feel the sparks. And every now and then there would be thunder.

Violet Deever had started it all when she said how hard it would be for Miss Nola Mae to climb all those stairs to the apartment over the drugstore, once she and Mr. Harter were married. Now Mr. Harter and Miss Nola Mae were off to one side on a wooden bench. They were practically back to back, one sitting at one end of the bench and one at the other.

WHO KIDNAPPED THE SHERIFF?

The dark cloud had spread over everybody. My brother, E.J., and his girlfriend, Gloria, were lying on the grass, but looking in different directions.

Mom and Dad had been holding hands until Dad said he had to go back to the newspaper office and finish up some work. Then Mom pulled her hand away and stared at him.

I hadn't wanted to bring Deever to the party, but Mom had insisted.

"The child's a visitor in our home," Mom said. "She's got no mother and she's got a father who ought to be in jail and probably is. She will be treated like family as long as she stays." There was a zip in her voice. It was there again as she talked to Dad.

"You promised to take me to Pete's Tavern for a hot roast-beef sandwich," she said. He smiled, shrugging his shoulders.

"I'll be home as early as I can," he said, and walked away, though you could see he didn't want to.

Deever was smiling at me. "Surely is nice that *we* aren't fighting," she said.

Jenna Jones glared at her, then snapped her head around and looked at me. "Especially on *my* birthday," Jenna said, too softly for Deever to hear. "Are we still going to the movies?"

"Sure," I said. I still hadn't bought her a birthday present.

"Sure, what?" asked Deever.

"Then, maybe it's time for me to go home and get ready," said Jenna.

"I'll walk you," I said.

"I'll walk you, too," said Deever. She stood up and brushed blades of fresh-cut grass from her knees.

"I don't think that'll be necessary," I said. But before we had a chance to argue about it, Mr. Harter called me over.

"You check on the flowers for the church yet, Pat?"

Miss Nola Mae lifted her eyes and stared at him.

"Won't be needing any flowers," she said. "Too many stairs." She stood up and walked toward the street.

"Nola Mae?" Mr. Harter called to her, but she didn't even turn around. Mom walked after her. Then Mom turned and called to Deever.

"You want to come with me, Violet?"

"I'll stay with Pat," Deever said. "He needs me."

I did not!

"You know what she wanted to do, Pat?" Mr. Harter asked.

"Me and Jenna are in a pretty big hurry, Mr. Harter."

"Me, too," said Deever.

"She expects me to live in *her* house. I lived upstairs over the drugstore for fifty years. She and I agreed that's where we would live. Now she says she's too old for all those stairs."

Deever was smiling brightly. She was the one who had first raised the idea about the stairs. Now the marriage was off, but she was smiling.

"Don't you think she's too old for all those stairs?" Deever asked.

"I don't know." He shook his head side to side. "She looks like a strong woman." He shook his head some more. "Maybe we weren't meant to get married after all, Pat. Maybe folks our age ought to settle for the good times we've already had." Then he smiled and put his hand on my shoulder.

"I know what we'll do, Pat. I'll write her out a pretty card and you can run over and bring it to her and see what happens."

"We got to go to the movies."

"Sounds like a good idea to me," said Deever, smiling brightly.

Jenna glared at her. We went inside the drugstore.

"How about this one?" Mr. Harter held out a fancy card. On the outside a young guy waved at a young girl. *"Hey, good-looking!"* he was saying. "Think she'd like this one?" Mr. Harter asked. He opened it. On the inside it said: *"What's cooking?"* He pulled a pen out of his pocket and wrote a few words, then handed the card to me.

"Thank you, Pat. I'll be waiting here just in case she has a message she wants you to bring back."

Deever was jumping all around. But Jenna wasn't smiling at all.

68

"But Jenna," I explained, "they are supposed to get married next weekend. And now maybe they're going to call it off. I don't want to go way over there, but I figure maybe I'd better."

"We'll never make it to the movies on time now," she said softly.

"Maybe just Pat and I could go," said Deever. She reached out for my sleeve, but Jenna grabbed my arm and pulled me her way.

"Jenna, you want to come with me to Miss Nola Mae's? We could go straight to the movies from there?"

"I don't think I would care to, Pat." Her voice wasn't quite as soft as it had been.

Deever just stood there, grinning.

"I could come back and maybe we could go to the second show," I said.

Jenna turned her back and walked away. I didn't know if it was a yes or a no.

"She's mad at you, Pat," said Deever, as soon as Jenna was out of hearing distance. "Do you really like her? She's kind of a toad, don't you think?"

I went to check the flowers first. Deever tagged along, but I didn't say a word to her. Let her stew.

Mr. Finley's grocery sells flowers for weddings and funerals. He said to tell Mr. Harter not to worry. Everything was ready and waiting. He even showed me where he kept the flowers in the cold-storage food locker. They were surrounded by sacks of onions and sides of beef.

"Somebody's going to have to spray the flowers with perfume before the wedding," Deever said as soon as we got outside.

The walk to Miss Nola Mae's was a hot one, and she was a long while answering the door. When she finally opened it, she stood there, brushing at her nose with a red handkerchief. Until that minute, I never thought of her crying a single tear in her whole life. But she'd been crying, all right.

"Well, Pat and Violet," she said in a cracky voice. "Didn't expect to see you again so soon."

I held out the fancy card to her. She stared at it. Then she reached for it. "Come on in. Heat don't get you, the mosquitoes will."

We sat in her living room while she read the card. Then she blew her nose in the red handkerchief again. She sat up straight and smiled at us.

"I'd really like to send a message back to him. Would you mind?" She didn't wait for us to answer. She bent down, wrote a few words on a piece of paper, and held it out. Deever grabbed it and smiled. I grabbed it from her and smiled even bigger.

The note said: "I guess the stairs won't bother."

"It's a code," Miss Nola Mae said. "He'll understand."

Deever started to say something, then looked at me and clamped her lips shut. The clock on the wall told me that if I was going to make it to Jenna's on time, I would have to start running.

When I gave the note to Mr. Harter, he put on a

big smile, headed for the telephone, and even forgot to say thank you. That wasn't the worst of it. The drugstore clock had a different time on it. I had missed the first show by a mile. I headed for home.

"It's a shame you won't make it on time, Pat," Deever said. It sounded like she was real pleased.

E.J. and Gloria were sitting on the front-porch swing. There was yelling going on.

"That's not what I said at all!" said E.J. Then he saw me and didn't say anything more. I went inside. Mom was in the living room, reading one of her books about creatures from outer space. She folded a corner on her page and smiled at Deever.

"Hi, sweetie," she said. She turned to me. "Pat, there's a phone message for you on the blackboard. And there's supper for you and E.J. and Violet on the stove."

The message was from Jenna. "The second show will be quite all right," it said.

Deever walked in the kitchen just as I was rubbing out the message.

"I saw that," she said, grinning. "Why do you want to go see an old *Mummy Returns* movie?"

"None of your business," I said. I followed her back into the living room. She went over and sat on the arm of Mom's chair.

"Mom, what time is it?" I asked.

"Is your father home yet, Pat?"

"I just got home myself. You know what time it is?"

71

"He promised he would come home early, and we would go to Pete's Tavern and have hot roast-beef sandwiches. You know how much I like them, Pat." She looked at her wristwatch. "It's not early at all. It's late." She turned back to her space-creatures book without telling me what time it was.

I called Jenna and told her about Mr. Harter and Miss Nola Mae.

"I'm not angry at you, Pat," she said. "Helping people is important. Come over as early as you can. It's supposed to be a scary movie. We don't want to miss the start."

The front door banged as I was putting the phone down. E.J. stomped into the living room.

"A little less noise, please," said Mom, lifting her head from her book and glaring. He glared back, but he began walking a less noisy walk.

Mom closed her book. "If we are going to eat supper late, I'm going to snack. Violet, would you like strawberry or vanilla ice cream?" She and Deever headed for the kitchen. Then Mom turned back to E.J.

"Would Gloria like some ice cream and cake?"

"She would not!"

"Does that mean the two of you are fighting again?"

E.J. marched out of the living room and into his bedroom. He closed the door sharply.

"Mom, I'm going to get Jenna and we're going to the movies."

"Why don't you take Violet with you, Pat? You'd like to go, wouldn't you, dear?"

"Mom!"

Deever ignored me. She nodded solemnly to Mom's question, then turned and walked toward the kitchen. She stopped in the doorway, watching me.

"Maybe I don't have time for ice cream," she said.

"Pat," Mom called from the kitchen, "would you stop at the newspaper office on your way and tell your father that it's not early. It's late. Just tell him that. Nothing more."

I checked the clock in the hall. There was time to do it, but I wasn't keen on it.

"We can do it, Pat," said Deever.

"Couldn't you phone him?" I called to Mom.

"The office phone is always busy. Besides, I don't want to *talk* to your father, dear. I merely want him to get the message I gave you."

Deever and I started toward the newspaper office with Mom's message. Then, only a block away, standing on the corner, arms folded across her chest, was E.J.'s girlfriend, Gloria. I kind of waved and tried to walk by, but Gloria wouldn't get out of the way.

"Where is that brother of yours?"

"Home."

"I thought he would come after me. It was his fault. He ought to be the one to say he's sorry."

73

"I'm in kind of a hurry, Gloria."

"No, you aren't," said Deever.

"Does he treat *all* his girlfriends like this?" Gloria was a pretty blond when she wasn't angry. Right now she didn't look so pretty.

"Would you do me a favor?" she asked.

"Certainly," said Deever.

"Would you go back and tell him something for me?"

I glared at Deever, daring her to answer. She smiled pleasantly.

"I wish I could," I told Gloria, "but my mother sent me to the newspaper office with a message for my father. I'm late now."

"Would you do it afterwards? It's terribly important."

If I had to go back home before I went to Jenna's, I would be in big trouble. This was turning out to be a night full of problems, and mine were fast becoming worse than anyone's.

"All you have to do is tell him . . ." She paused. "All you have to do is tell him I'm sorry. I'm really and truly sorry. Ask him to *please* call me later. Will you do that?" Her face was soft and pretty again.

The minute we got out of hearing distance, Deever stopped and grabbed my arm.

"Gross," she said. "She's another toad. Your brother isn't any better at choosing girls than you are."

74

When we got to the *Tickfaw Chronicle* office, Dad was on the phone.

"Dad!" I tried to get his attention, but he motioned me to sit and wait. He was talking to someone about ink and paper and it didn't sound too interesting. I found something to write a note on and put down what Mom had said and laid it on his desk.

He caught my eye, smiled at the two of us, and went back to his conversation. Then, as I reached the door, he told the party on the phone to hold, and called to me. I turned. He was taking a large white bag out of his desk drawer.

"Tell your mother there are hot roast-beef sandwiches in this bag for everybody. Tell her to keep my sandwich warm."

I took the bag and started to run.

When I knocked on Jenna's door, her father opened it.

"Hello, Patrick." He smiled. He is a tall, thin man and one of the nicest teachers at Jefferson School. "Jenna says to tell you the second movie started ten minutes ago."

"And tell him I'm not home and I don't want to talk to him. And tell him *nobody* brings another girl with them when they pick up their date. And tell him he can just leave the birthday present in the white bag on the hall table." Jenna was shouting from somewhere inside the house.

"I guess you heard all that," her father said, still

smiling. He waited for me to hand him the bag of hot roast-beef sandwiches, but I didn't do it because it wasn't the kind of a birthday present Jenna would have appreciated.

"Goodbye, then, Patrick." He closed the door gently.

I hadn't planned it this way. I really wanted Jenna to have a special birthday.

When we got home, E.J. was on the phone talking to Gloria.

"It was my fault. Please forgive me?" he asked. There was a pause. "Good!" he said.

"Ribbit! Ribbit!" said Deever, trying to sound like a toad.

There was another pause. "What? Pat? Yes, he's standing right here with a dumb look on his face." He handed me the phone.

"Here," he said. "She wants to talk to you."

Now I was in even more trouble. I had forgotten to give E.J. Gloria's message.

"Pat?" her voice purred. "Just listen, all right? Don't say anything." I nodded. "Pat, are you there?"

"Yes."

"Don't give E.J. the message I gave you. All right?"

"All right."

"Don't tell him I said I was sorry. He thinks it was his fault. You understand what I'm saying?"

"Yes."

"Good. Now let me talk to E.J. again."

Mom was back in the living room, reading her space-creatures book. I handed the warm white bag to her. Her face brightened. She sniffed and knew right away what was inside.

"That wonderful man!" She opened the bag and reached quickly inside.

"Come on into the kitchen with me, child," she said to Deever. "Would you like a glass of cold milk with your sandwich?"

I glared at Deever. Not one soul had asked me if I wanted one of those hot roast-beef sandwiches. I wouldn't even be hungry if they did.

"Dad said to keep his sandwich warm," I told Mom. She looked at me and smiled. It was what I call her hungry smile. It told me that if Dad didn't come home pretty quick, there wouldn't be any sandwich to keep warm.

I went to my bedroom. I pulled the pillow off my bed and hugged it. I wasn't one bit sleepy, but I got ready for bed anyway, lay down, and closed my eyes. The pillow was full of lumps.

There was a soft knock on the door.

"Pat?"

It was Deever.

She opened the door slowly and came in. She had a brown-gravy mustache from the roast beef. I didn't know whether to tell her to wipe her mouth or not.

"Pat, thank you for the sandwich," she said.

77

What could I say? It was my dad who bought it.

"Actually, Pat, I wanted to talk to you about something else. I really like living in this house."

"So?" Somebody had better remember whose house this really was.

"Want a glass of warm milk with vanilla and sugar in it?" she asked.

A few minutes later, we were sitting at the kitchen table, not saying a word. She took a sip of warm milk and smiled. Now she had a warm-milk mustache.

"You really tried hard to help everybody," she said.

I didn't have anything to say to that. It was true.

"You fixed things up for Mr. Harter and Miss Nola Mae. E.J. and Gloria are talking again. And your mom and dad, too." She took another sip of milk. "That's nice," she said.

"But Jenna's mad as heck at me, and Deever, it's mostly your fault."

She finished off the milk and put the glass down.

"Don't you worry, Pat. I've got it all figured)ut," she said. She went over to the cupboard and came back with the white sandwich-bag.

"I kept it clean," she said. "Tomorrow I'll help you find a birthday present to put in it."

I took the bag. She had smoothed it out. I nodded. For a change she was doing something nice.

"But you're wasting your time, Patrick," she said, "because Jenna's still a toad."

The
Television
Caper

My dad's a nice guy, most of the time. But he doesn't like being interrupted when he is working, and when the *Tickfaw Chronicle*'s weekly deadline gets near, sometimes he is close to mean.

I showed Violet Deever the advertisement. Then I went over to show it to Dad. He glared at me and Deever from under those bushy eyebrows.

"What do you two want?" His lips were drawn tight in a straight line.

"We were looking at the copy for the Waguespack store advertisement. He's running a special on televisions. A twenty-five-inch color set for only five hundred dollars."

Dad smacked his pencil down on the desk, and his lips curled into a grin.

"Let me see that!"

I gave him the ad. The television set looked beautiful in the picture.

"Lord, Pat, look at it," he said. He took his time reading the ad. His eyes moved from me to the ad. "I wonder how many he's got for sale?" I was pretty sure Dad was wondering if one would be left for him.

He had forgotten all about his work. Now he was smiling. His hand reached for the phone, then drew back. He glanced up at me, and his smile faded a bit.

"You going to stand there all day? Get back to your homework, or whatever it was you were doing." He was trying to sound angry.

I went back to our worktable. I grinned at Deever, but I didn't let Dad see my face. When I had gotten rid of the grin, I looked over at him. His hand was still on the phone. He wanted to call the television store. Then he saw me looking, and he moved his hand and went back to work. At least, that's what he wanted us to think he was doing. But I knew different. He and I were both thinking the same thing.

Mom wasn't going to let him have that brand-new, twenty-five-inch color television set, no matter what the cost.

At the supper table, I waited for him to mention something about Mr. Waguespack's ad. He was a long time doing it.

"Mary Dorothy, these are the best mashed potatoes I ever tasted in my whole life." He smiled at Mom, and she smiled back and pushed the bowl closer to him.

He also had something nice to say about the roast beef and the peas and the dessert, and by the end of the meal all of the food was on his end of the table.

When Mom stood up to bring the dishes into the kitchen, Dad hopped up, too. She looked at him out of the side of her eye, but she didn't say anything at first. Then she slowly sat down, and her hand lightly touched her forehead.

"This *has* been an exhausting day," she said, smiling first at him and then at me and Deever.

"Why, Mary Dorothy, you just sit right there. Pat and Violet and I will have this table cleaned in a jiffy," said Dad.

So the three of us ended up in the kitchen, with Dad washing and us wiping, and when every single dish and spoon was wiped and dry and put away, we went into the living room. Mom was reading a book about reincarnation. Dad sat on the sofa across from her. They smiled back and forth. Then Dad leaned forward and clasped his hands.

"Mary Dorothy," he said.

"No television, Michael," said Mom, still smiling. "What?"

"I saw Waguespack's ad this morning. But I still don't want a television set in this house. Since we got rid of the old one, Pat has been doing his homework on time and reading books for a change. You and Violet and I have had some nice talks. And E.J. . . . well, at least he isn't just hanging around the house."

This wasn't the time to tell her, but my brother, E.J., now spends most of his time looking at television at his girlfriend's house.

"But Mary Dorothy —"

"Michael, if the world is coming to an end, the president will tell us over the radio when he talks to us on Saturday. Anything else worthwhile that television has to offer can be found at the public library. We agreed on this, Michael. You know we did." She was smiling, but her words weren't soft anymore.

"But, Mary Dorothy, I really miss watching the television news."

Mom stood up suddenly and walked out of the room. She returned a second later with her arms loaded and walked over to Dad.

"Here is your nice, new robe." She handed it to him. "Here are your comfortable slippers." She put them on the floor at his feet. "And here is a brand-new Agatha Christie mystery I got from the library especially for you." She smiled at him, then walked back to her chair and sat down. She opened up her book and laid it in her lap. She looked across at Dad.

"That ought to make us almost even for all the nice things you said about my supper," she said.

The next morning Deever and I went straight to the newspaper office, and that's when I learned about the Lions Club raffle.

Mr. Claiborne Broussard was there, talking to Dad.

"The school needs an asphalt basketball court," Mr. Claiborne Broussard said, biting on his cigar. "Principal Joe Fairchild says he can't fit it into his budget, so I told him the Lions Club would help. We want you to give us some publicity in the *Tickfaw Chronicle*." Mr. Broussard was a heavy man, and the chair squeaked under his weight as he leaned to hand Dad a sheet of paper.

"You got it," said Dad. He began reading the paper. Suddenly his eyes widened.

"You going to raffle a twenty-five-inch color television?"

"We're getting a deal from Waguespack's store. Two hundred fifty dollars. My road construction company will provide the asphalt and build the court at a cut rate. But we still have to sell maybe a thousand raffle tickets to make this thing go right."

There was a glitter in Dad's eyes. He was thinking about those television news broadcasts.

"I'll help all I can," Dad said.

When Mr. Broussard left, Dad sat there, tapping his fingers on the desk, like he was playing one-handed piano. Then he looked up at me. He didn't speak. Just looked. He was still thinking about something. Then he smiled the tiniest bit.

85

I grinned at him. He just wouldn't give up. Now he was wondering what Mom would do if he bought a raffle ticket and then won the TV.

"We're going back home, Dad." I walked toward the door, but Deever didn't follow.

"I'll be there in a little while," she said.

As I left, she was standing next to Dad, saying something in a low voice. Whatever it was, she had his interest.

At supper that night Dad tried something different. He didn't compliment Mom on her food one single time. He just took two helpings of everything. I didn't think he would be able to stand straight at the end of the meal, but he popped up again, as soon as Mom started clearing the dishes.

"We'll take care of the dishes, Mary Dorothy. You go read your book."

She didn't argue one bit. But when the work was done, and Dad sat down, Mom started talking before he did.

"Who do you think will win the television set?" she asked. "I certainly hope that it's someone who *truly* wants one, and not a family like us who *surely* doesn't." She smiled at Dad. "And how is that mystery novel coming, Michael?"

He shrugged his shoulders, settled back in his chair, and opened the book.

We didn't talk about the raffle much at home after that, but at the newspaper office, when Mom wasn't there, things were different.

"Pat, get me a list of business places in town that are selling raffle tickets," Dad said.

"Sure, but why?"

"Maybe we can run them with our story on the raffle." But I knew he wasn't going to do that. It would take up too much space, and it would be free advertising.

The whispering between Dad and Deever got to be a regular thing. I didn't catch on to what was happening until Saturday. Deever went out for a walk, came back, walked over to a file cabinet, and dropped something in one of the folders. Then she took a fast look at me, but I pretended I wasn't watching. After that, she walked over to Dad and said something, and then came back and sat with me at our worktable.

In the middle of the afternoon both of them went out, and I took a look in the file. There were a couple of dozen raffle tickets inside. That's what they had been conspiring about all along. Dad wasn't giving up, but I thought he was wasting his time.

When they got back, I said that if he planned on buying any raffle tickets, I'd be glad to get them for him.

"Thank you, Pat, but I don't think so. You want to buy some for yourself, that would be OK." He never did look me straight in the eye.

The decision was to hold the raffle drawing at the school, and about a week ahead of time, Waguespack's store delivered the TV set. Dad and a few of the other Lions Club members were there to set it up. They worked at it all morning but couldn't get anything on the screen that made sense, so they called an electrician from the club, and it turned out he didn't know much about TV, either. Finally, Mr. Waguespack himself showed up, and they got a kind of wobbly picture out of it.

"It's the weather that's causing it to work poorly," said Mr. Waguespack, like he knew what he was talking about. Then Deever went over and twisted something in the back of the set. It began working fine.

Several times when I was in the newspaper office by myself, I checked the file with the raffle tickets, and it was fatter each time. If he bought too many more, he would be paying more to take a chance on the set than it would cost him to go out and buy one.

"What are you doing in that file cabinet?"

I hadn't heard the door open. Deever and Dad stood there. Dad was grim-faced, holding tight onto the door.

I didn't have any excuse. I shut the file drawer and turned to him.

"You and Deever sure bought a lot of tickets," I said.

He snapped the front door shut, walked to his desk, and sat down. He stuck his hands in his pants pocket, pulled out another handful of tickets, opened a desk drawer and dropped them in.

"Son, I just can't seem to come up with a good enough reason for your mom why I like to look at the news on television." He smiled weakly. "You're pretty good at keeping secrets, aren't you, Pat."

I wanted to help.

"Probably the best," I said with a smile.

"Good. Tomorrow's the raffle drawing, and then it'll be all over."

I wasn't too sure about that. If he spent all that money and didn't win, nobody would know but the three of us, and it *would* be all over. But if he won, the real battle had only started.

The raffle was set for Sunday afternoon in the school lunchroom. One corner had been cleared of all but two tables. On one of them were punch and cookies. On the other was a ten-gallon fish tank, stuffed with ticket stubs.

Dad had told Mom that it was an important community affair and that she ought to be there, but she said she had some baking she would rather do. Then he said he would treat her to a hot roast-beef sandwich when it was over, and she changed her mind.

The room slowly filled with people. Mr. Claiborne Broussard elected himself master of ceremonies, and the speechmaking started. Principal Joe Fairchild thanked the Lions Club for their generosity in making the asphalt basketball court possible. Lions Club President Wilbur Finley invited everyone to sample the punch and cookies, and made certain they knew all those goodies had come from his grocery store. Even Mr. Claiborne Broussard's son Emil got up and asked everyone to vote for him in the coming Town Council election.

Mr. Claiborne Broussard finally asked for quiet, and then things began happening I hadn't expected. He looked around the room, his eyes finally settling on me.

"Come on up here, Pat, and help with the drawing."

I didn't want to go up there. My dad's name was probably on half the tickets in that fish tank. Who would believe it was just by chance if I pulled out his name? I glanced over at him. There was a smile on his face, and an even bigger one on Deever's face. They didn't seem to be worried about a thing.

I looked over at Mom. She didn't suspect a thing, but the chances that there would be a television set in her front room were improving by the minute.

"Come on, son, get a move on," said Mr. Claiborne Broussard. "We are anxious to find out who's going to win this brand-new color television."

Everyone was suddenly staring at me. I grinned in self-defense and reached into the tank, stirred the ticket stubs about, then selected one and pulled it out.

Mr. Claiborne Broussard quickly reached out a large, hairy arm and grabbed it. "Good job, son. Now you give it to me."

I did as he asked, but I had seen the name.

It wasn't my father's name.

It was my mother's!

Dad and Violet must have put *her* name on all those tickets. They were hoping *she* would win.

Mom's name was announced, and the crowd started cheering. It was hard to figure out what she was thinking behind the thin smile that was on her face.

I squirmed my way to where she was standing. People were laughing and shaking her hand. Dad worked his way over to her and took her arm.

"Congratulations!" he said, shouting above the noise.

"A miracle!" Mom said. "A heavenly miracle, considering I didn't buy a single one of those tickets."

She went over and looked at the television set. She turned it on and watched the picture for a minute. She looked at Dad, smiling all the while. Then she turned the set off and took Dad's arm.

"Let's go home, Michael," she said.

"First, let me go talk to somebody about delivering the television set," he said.

She pulled on his sleeve. "No," she said. "If it really is my television set, I'll handle that part later."

After supper, Dad helped with the dishes again. It was like he knew he had won, but wasn't too pleased about the way he had won. There wasn't any talk about the television set. In fact, for a whole week there wasn't any talk about it. No questions and no answers. It just stayed at the school. Mom had told Principal Fairchild she would be taking care of the matter, and that was good enough for him.

Dad had gone to the newspaper office and had taken Deever with him to do some filing. Mom was sorting and folding the fresh-washed clothes. I was just sitting there. I wanted to say something about bringing the television home. But I didn't have the nerve to do it. I also wanted to tell her that I hadn't been in on tricking her, but I didn't know if that would be proper. Dad had tricked her and she knew it, and she was doing the only thing she could think of to kind of even things up.

I stared at a little hole in the rug over in the far corner of the room. I knew I ought to be asking about the TV, but I couldn't get started.

"Are you *ever* going to bring the television home?" I finally asked. I lifted my head and looked at her.

She folded a towel and placed it in the towel pile.

"Let me answer your question with a question. What would you do if somebody forced something on you that you didn't really want?"

I didn't have an answer for that. It was quiet. Suddenly her eyes were smiling at me.

"The truth is that it wasn't the news that was causing a problem with us owning a television. It was the soap operas. I'm here most times by myself, and I was cramming my day full with them. So all of you are being deprived because of me. I don't like that feeling one bit."

She picked up another towel.

"But I've decided what to do." She gave me a wink. "Your father's birthday is coming up in two weeks. We'll keep him guessing until then. After that, a man as persistent as he is ought to be able to look at the news when he wants to.

"You're pretty good at keeping secrets, aren't you, Pat?"

My eyes smiled back at her. "I get a lot of practice around here," I said.

Later I excused myself to go to the newspaper office. Dad and Deever looked up as I came in the door.

"Anything?" Dad asked.

I shook my head side to side. I didn't say a single word about televisions, and I didn't say a single word about soap operas, either.

The Dog Who
Wanted to Sing

My dog Ezmerelda changed a bit after her two puppies were born. And come to think of it, my dad did, too.

Violet Deever and I were sitting on the bottom step, playing with the puppies. Dad was on the porch swing with Ez. Her head was in his lap. There was a frown on Dad's face. You could see he was thinking hard about something. Ez had a plain old hound-dog look of pleasure on her face as Dad scratched her behind the ear.

"I'm going to do it!" he said. He stood up quickly, and Ez almost fell off the swing. "Mary Dorothy!" he yelled to Mom, and went inside. We chased after him.

"Mary Dorothy! Where are you? I'm going to buy that piano. I finally decided."

He had been wanting a piano for as long as I could remember. He would tell us how his father used to come home from work at the sawmill and sit down and play before supper. I could hear him telling it again.

"It was relaxing for him, Mary Dorothy. It would be for me, too. We've got the extra money. What do you think?"

"It's a good idea," she said, smiling. "Maybe you can even teach Violet and me a tune."

Deever's face brightened.

"Oh, I already know how to play piano," she said.

Dad glanced at her, but his mind was someplace else. He went back outside and sat on the swing. Ez jumped back up there with him and put her head in his lap. They sat on the porch until way after dark.

The piano was delivered a week later. It was a shiny upright, and it just barely fit through the front door.

"Watch out! Watch out!" yelled the music-store man to his helper. The piano had almost flattened one of the little pups dashing across the front porch.

They rolled it into the corner of the living room where a lamp and chair had been. The music-store man straightened up and wiped his brow.

"Thank you for delivering the piano yourself, Mr. Arceneaux," said Mom. "Could I fix you a cup of coffee?"

"When the work is done," he said. He sat his tall, skinny frame down in front of the piano and spent maybe an hour and a half tuning it. At last he smiled, rippled his fingers across the keys, and drifted into "The Black Hawk Waltz." It's Dad's favorite. He even has a phonograph record of it.

"Your piano is in perfect shape," he said, and accepted the coffee.

When he had gone, Deever walked over and sat on the piano bench. She stretched a leg and put a foot on a pedal. Then she began playing a soft, pretty tune. Sounded to me like she was as good as Mr. Arceneaux.

Mom came walking in to listen.

"Why, child, that's beautiful," she said.

"My father taught me to play," Deever said. Then suddenly her eyes dropped and she went out on the front porch and sat by herself on the swing. Deever had been with us in Tickfaw all summer long while her father was in New Orleans. We didn't talk much about him, but every now and then she would go off by herself, and I knew she was missing him.

After a while Mom and I went out on the porch to wait for Dad. Mom wanted to sit on the swing with Deever, but Ez was sprawled out with her head in Deever's lap and wouldn't move, so Mom sat on the steps with me.

Dad usually comes walking home at an easy pace, spends a few minutes on the porch with Ez, then goes inside and washes up for supper. This time he came home at a trot, smiling big.

"Is it here?" he called, when he was within shouting distance, and when Mom nodded yes, he quickened his pace. He took the steps two at a time, and was in the front room in a wink. Ez and I had been standing there, waiting to say hello, but he didn't pay any attention to either of us.

He stood in front of the piano and just stared and grinned for a long while. Then he reached over and stroked the new piano bench, like it was a friend.

He sat down to play. I'd never heard the tune before, but it was a mighty pretty one. He turned his head and smiled with pleasure at Mom.

And then it started. It sounded almost like a cat was trapped inside the piano and wanted to get out.

Dad stopped playing right in the middle of the tune.

"My Lord! It's a brand-new piano!"

But it wasn't coming from inside the piano. It was Ezmerelda, sitting out in the front yard, singing her head off. I guess she thought she knew the tune. Deever stood to one side, smiling.

When Dad realized it was only Ez, the relief showed plainly on his face. He went to the door.

"Shut up, Ez," he said with a laugh. "You gave me a scare."

He went back and sat down again. "Now, I'm going to play my favorite," he said, and I knew he was going to give "The Black Hawk Waltz" a try.

But he hadn't hit too many notes before Ez started singing again, and this time Dad got up mad and went stomping toward the front door. When Ez saw the look on his face, she didn't wait around to find out how he felt about her singing. She dashed under the front porch where he couldn't get at her.

"Pat, you tell *your* dog to be quiet," Dad snapped. "I can't play if that dog is going to do all that howling every time I strike a note! I've been waiting for this all day."

Ez was only *my* dog when she needed to be fed or rid of fleas. The rest of the time she was *his* dog.

"Maybe you can try again after supper," Mom said. "It's a strange sound for her. Dogs react to sound differently than we do."

"Well, I'm starting to react to certain sounds differently myself," he said. He sat down and began to play again, but he didn't get any farther than before. Ez's voice boomed up through the floorboards and almost drowned him out.

He glared at me, then went outside and bent down and threw a stick under the porch, but he missed.

"Michael, come on back in the house," said Mom. "We'll eat supper and then you can play some songs for us. I've got a nice roast and it's getting cold."

"I'm going to call Arceneaux first," Dad said. "Maybe he'll have some ideas."

A few minutes later he came into the dining room and pulled his chair out with a scrape.

"He thinks he's a comedian," Dad said. "His first idea was to get rid of the dog." Dad sat down and began helping himself to the potatoes. "And his second idea was to get some earplugs." He was smiling faintly.

Deever gave a laugh. "Then you couldn't hear what you were playing," she said.

"He meant earplugs for the dog." His smile broadened and he winked at her.

"Mr. O'Leary, you think Ez likes the music, or does it hurt her ears?" Deever asked.

"Violet, it would be a terrible blow to my ego to think that *my* dog didn't like *my* music. Some dogs like to sing, that's all."

After supper Mom told Dad about Deever's playing the piano, and we listened to her for a while.

"I haven't played in a long time," she said. "Would it be all right if I practice once in a while?"

Dad smiled and nodded.

"Anytime you like," he said. She thanked him and went outside.

When Dad sat down for his turn, he was a little fidgety. We hadn't heard from Ez yet. She must've been off someplace. But he hadn't sounded half a dozen notes before the dog started singing again. This time Dad decided it was going to be a contest to see which one could last the longest. The two of them made music together until bedtime.

"I'm not having as much fun playing this piano as I thought I was going to. Tomorrow some changes are going to be made."

In the morning he walked over to the piano and hit a single note, but Ez mustn't have been listening because nothing happened.

When Dad was leaving for work, I walked out on the porch with him. Ez was sitting in the swing, tail barely thumping back and forth. Dad glared at her.

"Pat, I got plenty to do at the newspaper office. You and Violet find time to check with the veterinarian. He's got to know something about why dogs howl when they hear music."

But he didn't.

"I've seen dogs run and hide from thunder and lightning," the veterinarian told us. "But that might be just the weather, and not the sound. And I knew one that would run and hide whenever his owner would play the violin. But I didn't like that man's violin playing, either." He opened a file cabinet. "Look here. I checked Ez out stem to stern less than a year ago, and there's nothing wrong with her ears. You tell Michael that I don't know why

some dogs howl when they hear music. I read somewhere a dog hears sixteen times more than a man
hears. Think of that."

But that wasn't a very helpful answer. "How do
you stop a dog from howling?" Deever asked.

"You can take a stick to 'em," he said.

"Dad would never beat Ezmerelda," I said.

"Then you tell Michael maybe he should practice more on that piano."

Everybody thought it was funny. And when I saw
Mr. Finley at the grocery, he thought it was fun-
niest of all. When he got through laughing, he told
us about a friend of his who had a hunting dog who
was afraid of the sound of a gun.

"So he tied him to a tree and shot off a box of
shells into the air. That dog got used to the noise
after a while."

"But guns aren't pianos, Mr. Finley."

"Didn't say they were," he said. He chuckled and
walked back inside the store.

We stopped off at Harter's Drug Store to see if
Mr. Harter had any part-time work for Deever to
do. Jenna Jones was sitting at a table right near the
door, sipping on a soda straw.

"Hello, Pat." Her eyes flicked to Deever and
then back to me. She took another slurp on the
soda, then pushed it away from her.

"I've been waiting for you to call," she said.

I knew she was going to say that, but the truth is,
I've been busy.

"I've been kind of busy," I said.

Her eyes moved back to Deever. "I see," she said. She stood, walked slowly to the front door, softly opened it, then closed it behind her.

I had meant to call. Maybe I could do it tomorrow.

Mr. Harter didn't have any work for Deever, but he had some news. "The wedding's off again," he said. He and Miss Nola Mae Miller had been planning to get married since the start of the summer, but they kept fighting and postponing the wedding. "I can't please that woman," he said. "I call her on the phone five times a day and she wants to know why I don't call her six times."

The minute we got outside, my mind was back on Ez.

"I'm getting worried, Deever. Dad hasn't said it yet, but it's getting close to where he's going to want to get rid of the dog or the piano. I raised that dog from a pup, and now I'm raising her pups."

"You want me to tell you what I've been thinking?"

"No."

"I was thinking maybe you could charge people money to hear Ez sing." Then she started giggling, and I turned my back on her and walked away.

Deever was practicing on the piano when Dad got home. Ez and I were on the porch swing, listening. Dad grunted something at the two of us and passed us both by.

He waited patiently until Deever stopped practicing. The minute she went outside, he marched straight to the piano, sat down, and began to play. Ez hopped down off the swing, stuck her head in the air, and began to sing. Then she heard Dad stomping across the floor toward the door and she jumped off the porch and hid underneath.

"Pat," he said, like I knew he would sooner or later, "it's either the dog or the piano, and I already paid too much money for it to be the piano. You find somebody to give that dog and her pups to."

"People don't take grown dogs with pups."

"People don't keep dogs that howl every time somebody tries to relax a little bit playing their piano."

He looked around. Deever had come inside and was somewhere with Mom.

"I don't want to make an issue of this, Pat, but with Violet practicing all the time, I can't even get to my own piano when I want to. Then when I do, that dog starts howling."

I didn't want to give away Ez. All that dog was doing was having a little fun.

"I'll tell you what I'll do," Dad said. "I'll set a regular practice time for myself. And maybe we should set a regular practice time for Violet, too. When I'm practicing, Violet can take Ez on a long walk. She likes the dog's company. Maybe that'll work out."

But when I told Deever that she would have a regular schedule for her practice, and would have to take Ez for a walk every day, she didn't think it would work at all.

"It's his piano, but I don't like schedules. If I *have* to practice at a certain time, and if I *have* to take Ez walking at a certain time, that's going to take all the fun out of it." She went outside and began whispering in Ez's ear.

I talked to Dad some more later.

"Violet's not too keen on all the scheduling," I said.

"How keen is she on playing *my* piano?" he asked.

"Maybe we could train Ez not to sing," I said.

"How you going to do that?"

I told him what the veterinarian had said about using a stick.

"I don't approve of beating dogs. I've never used a stick on you, either, if you'll just remember."

I started to tell him Mr. Finley's story about how they train gun-shy dogs, but I stopped because it didn't seem to make much sense. And then suddenly it did.

"You want to try an experiment?" I asked.

"Now, what does that mean?"

"Tomorrow's Saturday and you'll be home all day," I said. "The experiment starts at nine in the morning."

"You going to tell me what it is?" He was smiling now. It was starting to be a game.

"I got to make the arrangements first."

He kept the smile on his face, but there wasn't any smile in his words.

"All right, Pat, I'll suffer that hound one day longer. But I'm not fooling. Either something changes, or Ez will have to go."

Deever came out, wanting to know what was going on, but I didn't tell her. So she went over and sat with Ez and whispered in her ear.

"What are you doing?"

"Never you mind what I'm doing, Patrick O'Leary."

"Deever, all you'll get from whispering in a dog's ear is fleas up your nose."

She stopped whispering and stared at Ez's ear. Then she turned to me.

"I just don't want to have to practice according to a regular schedule," she said.

"So, why are you whispering to Ez?"

"For me to know and you to find out," she said.

I called up Mr. Arceneaux at the music store and told him my idea for the experiment. He said it sounded like a real dumb idea but that he was willing to help.

I went and told Mom about company coming, and she said she would make extra coffee and some biscuits.

Then I told Deever to stay close because I was going to need her help. "I'm not helping if you're not telling," she said. But I knew she would.

In the morning, Mr. Arceneaux stopped on the porch long enough to take a close look at Ez and scratch her behind the ears before coming into the house.

Dad looked sharply at me when Mr. Arceneaux arrived, but he quickly turned his attention to being a good host.

"I welcome your visit," he said. "But I want you to know I don't have the slightest idea what's going on around here."

"We are going to have a piano marathon," I told him.

"What?"

"That's what I said, too," said Mr. Arceneaux. "But the boy might have a good idea."

I told Dad about shooting the guns to train the hunting dog.

"We can do the same thing with the piano," I said. "You and Mr. Arceneaux and Deever can play piano all morning long, one after another. Ez is a smart dog. Sooner or later she's going to get the idea and shut up."

There was a sparkle in Dad's eyes.

"You are putting folks to a lot of trouble to save your dog, Pat," he said. "But this ought to be an enjoyable morning. Who will go first?"

"It's your piano," said Mr. Arceneaux.

Dad walked over to the screen door and took a look outside. Ez was nowhere to be seen. He sat at the piano and began playing his first song.

From somewhere outside, Ez began singing her first song.

Dad shuddered but kept on playing. Mr. Arceneaux laughed softly, but stopped when Dad turned his head to glare.

He played for about fifteen minutes, with Ez howling with him note for note. It was nice, soft, popular music.

"Somebody else better take a turn," he said finally.

Deever decided on ragtime. The music hopped around the room, and everybody was smiling, and then suddenly I realized that Ez wasn't singing. Then everyone else realized it, too.

Deever stopped playing ragtime and started in on some of the popular tunes Dad had been playing. But not a sound out of Ez.

"Maybe she just don't like your music, Violet," Mr. Arceneaux said with a grin.

At the end of another fifteen minutes, Mr. Arceneaux took over and played fancy classical music that would probably never be played on our piano again. Still no singing from Ez.

"You think she learned already?" asked Dad. Mom filled up the coffee cups, and there was a little talk about the election, and then Dad sat down to take his turn. He hadn't hit three notes when Ez started howling again. And she kept at it as long as he played.

"That's a very special dog," said Mr. Arceneaux. "She only sings for her master."

Then the three of them tried fooling Ez. One would play a bit. Then another would sit down and pick up the same tune. But Ez only sang when it was Dad who was playing.

"I wonder how she does that?" Mr. Arceneaux asked.

I told him what the veterinarian had said about how good a dog's hearing was.

The men downed their coffee. Then Mr. Arceneaux stood up. "Good coffee and good biscuits," he said. "But I got to go. We aren't going to be able to help you train your dog," he told Dad. "If a piano marathon will do it, you're going to have to do the marathoning all by yourself."

When he had gone, Dad shook his head and looked at me.

"I can't sit here all day long playing this piano, Pat. That would take all the fun out of it. My fingers wouldn't take it. Neither would my seat."

He moved close to me and lowered his voice.

"You know somethng else, Pat? Violet's not sticking to her regular practice time. Whenever Ez's singing drives me batty and I leave the piano, she rushes over and begins playing. She's getting so much practice time that she's playing better than me."

I started not to tell him, and then I decided that I would.

"Dad, Deever's been whispering to Ez just before you start to practice. It's almost like she is telling the dog what to do."

He cocked his head. "Now, that doesn't make sense, son. People don't talk to dogs, even if it does look like the dog is listening. But maybe I need to talk to Violet."

When he called, she came in so innocent-looking, a mother would have trusted her with a newborn babe in the middle of an alligator swamp.

"Ez is a pretty smart dog," Dad said to Deever, and Deever nodded. "That dog does practically anything I ask her to do."

Deever nodded again. "Me, too," she said.

Dad's eyes kind of rolled. "Violet, child, have you been telling that dog to howl when I play piano?"

She smiled at him. "Why, Mr. O'Leary, people don't talk to dogs. At least, they don't talk to them about things like that."

"That's what I think, too, Violet. Just checking."

He moved off a ways and his voice softened.

"You know, I'm starting to wonder about myself. A grown man ought not to be thinking this way."

I was beginning to think the same thing. But what was going on around here?

When Deever went out in the front yard, I followed her. She went right straight to where Ez was lying under the shade tree.

"Deever, do you *really* know how to talk to Ez?"

She looked up at me, head twisted sideways, like she was figuring out whether she would answer or not.

"I've been thinking about that myself, Pat. And I've decided it's a lot more complicated than that."

"Somebody talking to a dog seems pretty complicated to me."

"But all I do is say the words, Pat. That's not much of anything. It's the fact that Ez *hears* the words that's the magic."

Suddenly I was looking at that dog with new respect.

Then I looked back at Deever. I couldn't tell what she was thinking, but there was a twinkle in her eyes, and I had seen it before.

"All this is a lot of silly talk, right?" I said. "You're after something. But maybe this time you won't get it."

"Maybe not," she said. "But there's been a lot less talk about *regular* practice and *regular* dog walking the last couple of days." She leaned over and gave Ez a kiss on the side of her head and whispered in her ear.

She wanted me to think that Ez's singing was her doing, but that was a lot of foolishness. Then suddenly Ez stood up, stretched, and walked slowly toward the house. She went under the porch steps and lay down, eyes wide open, like she was waiting for something to happen.

"All right, then, Deever, what did you say to her this time?"

She looked at me, head tilted sideways.

"You won't tell?"

"Promise," I said.

"Well," she said, "it's about time for your dad to start his piano practice. I thought Ez would like to be ready and waiting."

More foolishness.

In time, Ez stopped her singing. But I never did find out if Deever could talk to that dog.

Who Kidnapped the Sheriff?

The Sheriff got kidnapped on Friday afternoon. Dad was rushing around the office of the *Tickfaw Chronicle* like elephants were chasing him. I had been begging him to let me write some of the news stories for the paper, but he said I was too young. Now I saw my chance. He needed all the help he could get.

He was bent over his typewriter. He had the phone in one hand, talking loudly to somebody. With the other hand he poked at the typewriter keys with a single finger. I can type better than that.

Suddenly he slammed down the phone.

"Holy cow!" he shouted.

He straightened up his big shoulders and glared around the room. Mom sat at her desk in the corner, twitching a pencil in her hair. She wasn't paying him any attention. She never does when he yells about something.

"I called Tickfaw City Hall to find out what's happening, and you know what that durn-fool deputy sheriff said to me?"

Mom lifted her eyes from whatever she was typing and smiled.

"He said: 'I'm sorry, Mr. O'Leary, but everybody's out of town for the weekend.' "

He turned back to his typewriter.

"The whole town's out of town for the weekend. Imagine that."

His eyes moved to me. I hadn't done a thing, so I knew all I was going to get was a glaring.

"Patrick Wilson O'Leary! What's the worst word in the world?"

It was a game we played. He had asked me that question practically once a week for as long as I can remember. But he never seemed to get tired of it.

"The worst word in the world is *mean*," I said.

"You are right. And don't you forget it. I never met a meaner man than the Mayor of Tickfaw. He's hiding someplace because he doesn't want to talk to me. He knows something about the kidnapping, but he won't tell me."

Dad sounded madder than he was. He and the Mayor had been friends since they were kids. Both made all-state in high-school football. They still play a game of touch with us kids once in a while. We don't care for it too much because Dad and the Mayor want to run things their way all the time.

Dad went back to his one-finger typing.

"Could I help?" I asked.

The typing stopped. Dad glared again. He didn't like being interrupted.

"I can type pretty good." I looked from him to Mom. She smiled but didn't say anything. We had been through this before, and she had even been on my side the first couple of times.

"Pat," Dad said, "you're just not old enough. Let your mom and me run this newspaper for a while longer. Be content to help deliver the papers once a week." He reached for the phone and began to dial, still talking to me.

"Too much going on," he said. "The kidnappers want ten thousand dollars' ransom. The whole town's turned upside down. That lummox of a sheriff gets himself kidnapped a week ahead of the town's election. Before this there wasn't a chance he would've been reelected. But who's going to vote against a man who is kidnapped right when you are voting?"

I still wanted to help. The Sheriff is my friend. He lets me sit in the jail and answer the phone every once in a while. Nobody ever calls with anything important. I just tell the bill collectors he isn't there. He even takes me squirrel hunting. I'm getting good at sitting and waiting for squirrels to move.

"Got to outwit them squirrels," the Sheriff would say. "Got to do whatever you have to."

I sat at the desk in the back room where I do my homework. I shuffled some books around, but I just didn't feel like arithmetic.

I'm old enough to be a newspaperman. I know how to ask good questions, and I'm good at English, and I type pretty well. I sat there like that, talking to myself.

"Patrick O'Leary," I finally said to myself, "it won't do you a bit of good to sit here and feel sorry for yourself."

I decided to start thinking like a newspaperman. What did the Mayor know about the kidnapping that he wouldn't tell Dad? How could I find out?

"I'm going for a walk," I called, as I left the office.

"Good!" Dad replied, interrupting his phone conversation just long enough to give me a silly grin. He winked and I winked back. He was saying: "Don't go away mad," and I was saying: "I'm going to find out something you don't know."

I walked out into the summer heat and turned toward the Sheriff's office. I sat on the hard curb across the street and watched. People marched in and out of the one-story brick building. They hurried across the tiny dirt lawn where no grass ever grew. Too many things were happening for me to know what was *really* happening. I stood up and started across the street to find out. Halfway across I stopped. The Mayor had come out of the building. His arm was draped across the shoulders of Violet Deever!

That girl had a way of getting right in the middle of everything.

The Mayor stopped when he and Deever reached the sidewalk. He patted her on the shoulder and smiled broadly.

"Thank you for your help, young lady. If you hadn't seen what you did, we would be worse off than we are now. It's a shame you can't remember more about the appearance of the man." He gave Deever a final pat. "If we find him, we'll want you to take a look."

Deever nodded, turned, and walked away. I waited a bit, then followed.

At Main and Second, Deever turned left. At Second and Dodge, she turned right. When I made the turn, she was waiting.

"Hello, Pat. I'm going to my job at the drugstore. You can walk with me if you want to."

"Did you really see the kidnapper?"

"Why do you want to know?"

"I want to write a story for the newspaper, that's why."

"Is that a fact?"

I couldn't tell if she was really interested in me writing the story, or was just being smart.

"Your father lets you write stories for the *Tick-faw Chronicle*?"

"Sometimes." Maybe someday.

"Big ones? Front-page ones? The kind that make people famous?" The last time I saw that look on her face was when she showed me the trick with the shells and the pea and won all my money.

"Like what?"

"Like the kidnapping?"

"That's the story I want to write," I said.

"Well then, Pat, now there are going to be two stories. I'm the one that's got all the facts. I'm planning on being a newspaper reporter myself someday."

That wouldn't work at all. Two people writing the same story. Both of us kids. And Dad wasn't a bit interested in stories by kids.

"You going to tell me what the kidnapper looked like?"

She walked away, and I saw my chance to get a story published in the newspaper walk away with her, one long stride at a time. Suddenly she turned. Her dark eyes bored holes in me.

"What about partners?" she asked. I hadn't expected that. I stared at her. What was going on in her mind? She wanted to write the story all by herself. And so did I. I wanted to see my name sitting up there, under the headline. It would say: "SHERIFF'S KIDNAPPING SOLVED, by Patrick Wilson O'Leary."

Then I had another thought. Was she just trying to be nice? If that was it, she surely wasn't going to say it out loud. And, I did need her help to get the facts, just as she needed my help to get the story in the newspaper. I'd have to stay on my toes every minute to keep it fifty-fifty. But I nodded that partners was OK.

"All right, Pat. Ask me some questions." Deever folded her hands across her chest and smiled like she was somebody important and knew all the answers.

"What did he look like?" I began.

"Actually, Pat, he had a patch on one eye, and he wore horn-rimmed glasses, and he had long, white hair."

"Aw, you're joking."

"That's what the Mayor said, too, at first," she said.

"Well, we've got to do better than that. Did he look like any famous person?"

"What do you mean?"

"A movie actor?"

"Oh," said Deever. She thought about it. Then she smiled. "Maybe a little bit like Long John Silver, the pirate." She rippled with laughter. Then, when she saw I wasn't laughing along with her, she spun around and walked away. I hurried and caught up.

"Deever?"

"Actually, Pat, if you take away the eye patch

and the horn-rimmed glasses, maybe he looked a little bit like George Washington."

It was as close to a clue as I was going to get.

We decided to try to put ourselves into the mind of the kidnapper. Where would he hide the Sheriff? Probably someplace close by, but not right in town.

"There's a dozen abandoned barns and sheds and even farmhouses within ten miles of Tickfaw," I said.

"You have a bike?" she asked. I nodded. "Then you will just have to be the one to check them out. I have to work at Mr. Harter's drugstore."

For three days I pedaled my bicycle all over the place and got darned tired doing it.

"Maybe we ought to shift to another plan," I told her. "The kidnapper's got to eat, right? So, he's got to go to the grocery store. And maybe he needs gas from the filling station, and maybe he gets mail at the post office."

I took the grocery store first, because it was closest to the newspaper office. I sat on the curb outside and sweated until my butt was sore, and then I tried looking inside the store. There was hardly a strange face to be seen. To pass the time, I even tried drawing a picture of George Washington, and I didn't do too bad a job of it.

At the end of the second day, I decided there had to be a fatal flaw in our plan, although I didn't know what it was. I went to the drugstore to talk to Deever. I showed her the picture I had drawn.

"Are you sure this is the man you saw kidnap the Sheriff?"

"Actually, Pat, I never said I saw anybody kidnap the Sheriff. You are having the same trouble the Mayor had. I said I saw a mighty strange-looking man walk out of the Sheriff's office and head up the street. A couple of minutes later, the deputy comes running out the front door, yelling his head off. He had found the ransom note. I told them what I saw, and they figure it had to be the kidnapper."

"Oh, well, that's pretty much the same thing. I guess I'll go look some more. Besides, I want to see if that dumb-looking dog comes back to the grocery again tomorrow."

Deever's head jerked. "What dumb-looking dog?"

"It's a real ugly dog. This big guy with a limp comes to the grocery every day about noontime. He brings the ugly dog with him."

"What does the ugly dog look like?"

"He's got spots and flappy ears and a short tail. What kind of dog is that?"

"I don't know." Deever took my pencil and drew a picture on the back of George Washington.

"Look like this?" she asked.

"Pretty much," I said.

125

"Actually, Pat, I forgot to tell you about the dog."

This wasn't the right time for forgetting about important things.

"An ugly, spotted dog was following George Washington when I saw him come out of the Sheriff's office."

Shortly before noon the next day we plunked ourselves down on the curb across the street from the grocery store. It wasn't the best day for spotting strangers, because people were whizzing by like flies, heading for the election polling place at the public library. But we lucked out. The ugly dog showed up first, followed closely by the large man with the limp. Most of his face was hidden by a broad-brimmed hat.

"Pat! It looks like him!"

"But his hair's red! You said white!"

We sat there until the big man left the grocery. There was no hurry. He would walk to Main Street and then turn to the left or right. Those were the only two ways out of town. But when he reached Main he didn't turn left or right. He kept on going, heading for the far side of town. And only moments later, under the shade trees that lined the sidewalk, the limp disappeared.

It was when the man and the dog made a sudden turn into the walk of a white house set far back off the street that I realized what was happening. It was the very house the Sheriff lived in.

"We've got the kidnapper cornered," I whispered to Deever.

"Let's get closer where we can see," she whispered back.

I looked at her. We were head-to-head with a real live kidnapper. I didn't know how close I wanted to get. But she crept forward, and so did I. We knelt near an open window. We snuck a look in.

Somebody sat at the table with his back to the window. There was an empty chair across from him. Nobody else was in the room. On the table were a red wig and a white wig and a cane and a floppy hat. As I watched, the man removed a pair of dark glasses.

"Bunch of squirrels," the man said.

We lowered our heads and moved silently away.

"Pat, that's the Sheriff!"

And it was. The Sheriff had kidnapped himself!

"Why would he do that?" I asked Deever.

She eased up slowly and sneaked another look in the window. Then she knelt down.

"I can figure one reason," she whispered. "Your dad said nobody'd vote against a man who was kidnapped. Everybody's voting right this minute. Who you figure they'll vote for?"

We crept out to the road and down a bit where we couldn't be seen from the house.

"You're saying he did something dishonest, but he's my friend."

"I don't think there's a law against kidnapping yourself. But Pat, even if there was, any man smart enough to do it probably deserves to be reelected." She started up the road.

"Boy," she said, "do we have a story. Let's run to the *Tickfaw Chronicle* office. We'll write the story and get our names in the paper and become famous." She tugged at my arm to get me to move faster.

But I didn't want to move faster. I had some thinking to do. I told Deever about the Sheriff taking me squirrel hunting.

"That sounds like fun," she said. "Then suppose we don't tell them everything we know."

It was hard walking into the office without our faces giving the whole thing away. But Dad helped. He was so intent on what he was writing, he only gave us a grunt as we passed his desk. We made it to the little back room and closed the door.

I leaned back on the door. We were going to be newspaper reporters. It felt good. It was the kind of feeling you get when you know you are going on a picnic first thing tomorrow morning.

"Boy, this is going to be fun!" I told her.

"Right," she said. She walked over and sat behind the typewriter.

Dad had never given me a chance to prove that I could write a story for the paper. Now I was going to show him.

Deever sat there like she was waiting for something. She was still smiling, but not as big as before.

"What do we do now?" she asked.

"We write the story," I said.

"I can't type," she said.

"I'll type, Deever. You just think up what to say."

"Right."

"OK," I told her. "Start talking."

I sat there, looking at the keys, hoping she didn't talk too fast. I waited. I looked up at her.

"How do you think we ought to start off?" she asked.

"You are the one who is going to do the talking. I'm going to do the typing."

"Right," she said. I looked back at the keys, waiting.

"Actually, Pat, this is harder work than I thought it would be."

But we worked at it together, and the words finally came out. About an hour later the story was written.

"Let's go talk to my dad," I said. She looked as pleased as I felt.

He was punching away at the typewriter, brow furrowed. He raised his eyes and glared at our interruption.

"Me and Deever were wondering if you would like to see a really good story for your front page?"

He gave out a snort, lowered his eyes, and stabbed three keys hard enough to punch holes in the paper.

"I told you *no* last week and I'm telling you *no* right now. Pat, I'm sitting here writing a story about how the Sheriff got reelected, even while he is kidnapped, and I'm not enjoying myself. That big lummox has everybody in town feeling sorry for him." He looked up at me. His eyes softened. "I tell you what. If you worked hard on a story and want me to read it, I'll read it. Put it on my desk. I promise to read it before I go home tonight."

But it was kind of like he was just getting rid of us.

Then the phone rang. It was business. He grabbed his hat and headed for the door. "Pat, I'll be back in an hour. If you leave, lock the front door." He walked out.

I started to put the story on his desk.

"That's not the way! Tonight will be too late, Pat," said Deever. "Who knows what will happen by then? He's got to read that story in time to get it in the paper. Maybe I know a way."

We went back to the typewriter and made a few changes.

"Should we use our real names on it?" I asked.

Deever grinned. She took page one and put it in the typewriter. She punched at some keys. I read over her shoulder. Then it was my turn to grin. We

sealed the story in a large envelope. We went outside and locked the front door. Then I slid the envelope through the mail slot in the door like the
postman had delivered it. It would be waiting for
Dad when he got back.

Deever and I went to the drugstore, and she
treated me to a chocolate soda. It was hard to slurp
and smile at the same time. When enough time had
passed, we walked back to the newspaper office.
Inside, the Mayor stood in front of Dad's desk,
shaking his head side to side.

"Well," said the Mayor, "we rescued the Sheriff,
but we didn't get the kidnapper. We have the
house staked out, but he's not likely to return." The
Mayor stared hard at my father.

"What I want to know, Michael O'Leary, is how
you found out where the kidnapper was keeping
the Sheriff?"

"Mr. Mayor, I worked hard on this story. I put
myself in the place of the kidnapper and asked
where was the least likely place to keep the Sheriff.
And I got the right answer."

"You saying you figured it out all by yourself?"

"Well, maybe not all of it."

Dad smiled, lowered his head for a moment, then
lifted it and stuck out his chin.

"A newspaperman doesn't reveal his sources, Mr.
Mayor."

When the Mayor left, Dad stood up and walked

across the room to Mom's desk, shaking his head side to side. Mom was bubbling laughter through her fingers.

"Why, Mary Dorothy, I couldn't tell the Mayor I read the whole thing in a story written by George and Mary Washington. He'd laugh me out of town." He turned his head and glared at Deever and me. He stuck his finger out and jabbed it at us.

"I don't want a thing that's happened here to leave this room, you hear?"

"Actually, Mr. O'Leary," said Deever, "we wouldn't think of telling anyone. Was it a horrible mess of a story?"

Dad had gone back to his desk.

"No. Pretty well written. Didn't have to change hardly a word."

We started to leave.

"Just hold it up a minute," Dad said sternly. "Come back here and sit down." He sounded angry. I didn't know if I would like was was going to happen next. I sat down on one side of the desk, and Deever sat on the other.

He took a piece of paper out of his desk drawer and laid it flat in front of him.

"I decided to change my mind about certain things around this newspaper office," he said.

I was half listening to his words and half looking at the piece of paper on his desk. I was looking at it upside down, but there wasn't a doubt about what it was.

"Maybe it's time for me to share some of the work with you two."

What he had hold of was my picture of George Washington. He kept looking at it and smoothing it out with the palms of his hands. Then he turned it over and smoothed out the other side. There was Deever's picture of the Sheriff's dog.

"They're getting a new engine over at the fire station. I want you two to go over and talk to the chief. Let him tell you all about it. I'll get a picture tomorrow. We'll use your story and my picture in the next issue." He looked up suddenly and stared me square in the eye. Then his stare shifted to Deever.

"That OK with you two?" he asked.

He didn't have to ask twice. Deever grabbed hold of my arm and pulled me toward the door. Once we were outside, she kept tugging me along, smiling and jogging.

"Now, Pat, we are newspaper reporters," she said. Then she giggled. "Although nobody knows it yet but you and me." Suddenly she stopped. Her eyes twinkled. "I think we should tell someone." She began running again, pulling me along.

"Where we going?"

"Actually, Pat, I thought we could visit the Sheriff. Squirrel hunting sounds like lots of fun. I'm sure he'll be happy to teach me to hunt squirrel, once we have had our little chat."

The
Scavenger Hunt

Sometimes I like standing in the window of the newspaper office and watching Miss Alverna Dunkle. She does the same thing every Monday morning. She walks down the other side of the street until she gets just opposite us. Then she stands and waits until some little kid walks by. He stops. They talk. She gives him something. The kid turns and runs to the end of the block and goes in the candy store. In a minute he comes out with a bag and runs back to Miss Alverna. He hands her the bag. She reaches inside and hands something to him. Then she turns around and walks back the way she came.

Must be she doesn't want people seeing her buy all those peppermints every week.

I turned away from the window one Monday,

after watching Miss Alverna get her week's supply of candy. Violet Deever and I were helping Dad clean up the storage room at the newspaper office. It was hot, dusty work.

"What do I do with this box?" I asked Dad. I'd found it way back in a corner, and it smelled like mothballs.

"Won't know until we see what's inside," he said.

The cardboard cracked and tore when we opened it. It was a mighty old box.

"Lord," he said, "look at that!"

The first thing I took out was an old shoe. It had a metal buckle on it. I'd never seen a shoe like that before. He took it from me, smiling, holding it up.

"We had been on a scavenger hunt," he said. "I threw some of our prizes in the box to remember by."

I pulled out a book filled with poetry. Deever reached in and got a red beanbag, a picture of a horse, and a bleached seashell. On the bottom of the box was a magazine, yellowing with age. I lifted it carefully. Beneath it was a sheet of paper with writing on it. I read it aloud.

> *We, the Unholy Five, solemnly swear to hold a reunion twenty years from this date, to dine on hot dogs, straw-berry jumbo, and pistachio ice cream, and to share memories, good and elsewise.*

There were five signatures. I recognized my dad's and mom's right away. Then I realized I recognized two more. Miss Alverna Dunkle's name was there. Right next to hers was the name of Jonathan Bear, the man who owned the candy store.

"Who's this?" I pointed to the only name I didn't know.

"Oh, that's the Philosopher," said Dad. "He was sweet on your mom way back then." He paused. "Poor boy. He died from a heart attack when he was still a young man."

Slowly he put the things back in the box, the magazine first so that it would lie flat on the bottom. He piled the rest on top, but kept hold of the paper with the names on it.

"Sad to say, we'll never have that reunion. The Philosopher's gone. And Alverna and the Candyman haven't spoken to one another in twenty years."

Deever's head jerked up, but she didn't say a word.

We had finished cleaning the storage room and were on our way home for lunch when Deever stopped suddenly.

"Pat, why wouldn't one person talk to another person for twenty years?"

"Must be pretty mad at one another," I said. I told her about the way Miss Alverna buys her candy.

"Actually, that's very strange," she said. She

turned around and started back the way we came.

"Where you going?" I asked.

"The candy store."

"It's time for lunch." I was hungry.

"I'm going to find out why they don't talk," she said.

"Deever, that's none of your business."

"I'm doing it, anyway." She looked at me, but she wasn't asking me to come along. She didn't care whether I did or not. Before I could think of what to do, she crossed the street and pulled open the door to the candy store. I followed her inside.

The Candyman stood behind the counter, smiling. The whole store was one big pink-and-white smile, with dots of chocolate here and there. It was probably my favorite place in town. There was a single white table near the window for folks who wanted to sit and chat. A small white vase held two red roses. He put fresh ones in the vase every day. There were only two chairs. He told me once he didn't care for crowds of people in his store.

"Fresh out of pralines, Pat. Maybe I'll make some more this afternoon."

He knew my favorite. He was looking at Deever. He had seen her before, but he didn't know her name, so I told him.

He stuck out his hand and looked at her over the top of his rimless eyeglasses.

"Chocolate fudge," he said, grasping her hand firmly.

Deever gave a little smile, but pulled her hand away.

"Am I right?"

I didn't know what he was talking about, but she must have, because she nodded. The Candyman went behind the counter. He came back with a hunk of fudge in the middle of a paper napkin. He handed it to Deever. Then he saw me looking at him.

"Pat, I thought you knew I could read minds. Folks send out these waves. Especially kids. I can't read everything that's sent. I can only read the candy part." He turned to Deever again.

"And I was right, wasn't I?"

Deever was chomping on the fudge. She smiled and chewed. Then she swallowed the last tasty bit and wiped her mouth with the back of her hand.

"Why haven't you talked to Miss Alverna Dunkle in twenty years?" she asked.

"Deever!" I had hoped she would at least sneak up on the question, but that wasn't her way.

The Candyman didn't say a word. His arms were at his sides. He pulled them to his chest and kind of folded them. Then he dropped them, and they hung limp at his sides again.

I was waiting for him to tell us to get out of his store, but he didn't seem to know what to do. Finally, he turned and walked around the counter and into the kitchen behind the store, not saying a word.

"Let's go, Deever. You made him angry."

But all she did was walk over to the table and sit down.

"I'm not going anywhere, Pat. I'm going to sit right here until he comes back out." There was a fleck of chocolate fudge in the corner of her mouth and it made her look silly. She must have sensed it, because her tongue flicked out, and it disappeared.

It was maybe ten minutes before the Candyman finally came out. He seemed surprised to see us. He paused for a moment. Then he walked toward the table, and I stood up quick to give him a seat. He lowered himself into the chair like he was weary. He looked at Deever, then at me. Then he hopped up quick, walked behind the counter, and came back with two big hunks of chocolate fudge. We each got one.

"No charge," he said.

I nibbled at mine. Deever wrapped hers in the napkin for later.

"Why do you want to know?" he asked.

Deever told him what Dad had said about the scavenger hunt, and the paper with the signatures that promised there would be a reunion.

"The Unholy Five," he said. "That's what the Philosopher used to call us." He was sitting up straight, intent on his memories. His head was down, looking at the table. Then his head slowly came up, as if he had made a decision.

"Alverna and I were a twosome then. I loved her

dearly. The day of the scavenger hunt had been pure joy. We ran around holding hands and laughing all day long.

" 'Wouldn't it be nice to do this forever,' she said.

"I wanted to ask her to marry me right then and there, but my tongue was tied. When I got home, I sat down and wrote a letter. Hardest letter I ever wrote. When I finally got it right, I didn't have the nerve to deliver it. So I brought it to Pat's mom and asked if she would. She and Alverna were good friends. Your mom gave me a funny look, but she didn't even ask what was in the letter."

He was silent for a long time.

"So, what happened?" asked Deever. "Why did you stop talking? Did she turn you down?"

He raised his head and smiled faintly.

"No, she didn't turn me down. I sent her a proposal of marriage, and she didn't even answer. Not then, and not in the twenty years since."

When we thanked him for the candy, he didn't say good-bye. He sat there and stared at his hands lying flat on the table.

"OK, Deever," I said when we were outside. "Now, let's go get lunch. You found out what you wanted to know."

Her head snapped around. "You saying you didn't want to know why they weren't talking?"

I had wanted to know. But I guess I hadn't wanted to know bad enough to ask outright.

143

She began walking faster.

"Where are you going now?" I ran to catch up.

"To find out the rest of it," she said.

Miss Alverna Dunkle lived on one of the prettiest streets in town. Lots of trees and shade. Houses spread far apart, and sitting back off the street behind grassy lawns.

A big, dark Doberman pinscher lay on the front porch and watched us come up the walk. When we reached the bottom of the steps, he let out a low growl and showed teeth. We stopped. The dog didn't move. He just stared at us so we would know we weren't welcome. Then he stood and let out a single sharp bark, and I heard footsteps coming toward the front door.

The dog quieted down as soon as she opened the door. She stood there, tall, smiling pleasantly, wondering what we wanted. Miss Alverna Dunkle sold real estate, and visited Mom and Dad at the newspaper office every now and then.

Deever reached in her pocket and pulled out the piece of fudge wrapped in the napkin.

"It's from the Candyman," she said, offering it.

Miss Alverna had been standing there, quiet and in control. Suddenly she shuddered. Something changed about her. It wasn't anything you could see, but even the dog sensed it and growled softly. She didn't reach out to take the fudge.

"Perhaps you had better come inside," she said, almost in a whisper.

We walked through a dark front room filled with stuffed furniture and small, moody paintings on the wall. But the rest of the house was white — walls, ceiling, even the furniture. And the paintings were large, with splotchy, bright colors. I stopped in front of one and studied it. Lots of yellow, with red and blue swirling around like a storm.

"It's a hobby," she said, smiling. "I like the colors."

"What's it supposed to be?" I asked.

"That's a good question," she said. "Perhaps it's just supposed to be enjoyed."

She sat us at the kitchen table, and without asking, took soft drinks from the refrigerator and plunked them down in front of us.

"Now, tell me about the Candyman," she said, sitting down with us. She was still smiling, but I sensed the same thing I did when we were on the porch. It was like she was a flower vase made out of thin glass. If we said the wrong thing, she would shatter.

"We want to know —" Deever started to talk, but I said, "Let me do it."

She glared at me, but she stopped talking.

I didn't know what to say, but I knew that starting out slowly would be in the right direction, so I told her about finding the box of scavenger-hunt things, and the signatures on the reunion paper.

She listened carefully, and you could almost see the moment when she stopped being in the kitchen and went off into her memories. And then Deever jarred her back into the present.

"Why didn't you answer the Candyman's marriage proposal?"

"What?" But she had understood. Her face was expressionless, but her eyes darted back and forth between Deever and me. Then the pain began to show on her face again.

"But I did answer," she said. "I told him I loved him. I said yes. I put his letter and my answer in one envelope to send back to him. I knew we would want to keep those two letters forever." She brushed her cheek with the back of her hand. "But I was wrong," she said. "He changed his mind. He never spoke to me again."

We sat awhile, then said good-bye. The dog let us pass with only a low growl. When we reached the front sidewalk, I started running as fast as I could. Deever had a hard time keeping up.

"Pat, I'm getting angry," she yelled at me. "I don't like running on a hot day like this."

But the heck with her. I had run when *she* wanted to run. Miss Alverna Dunkle had told us she had given her answer to my mom to deliver to the Candyman. It had never reached him. I wanted to know why.

Mom was in the kitchen, wrapping plates in old newspapers. She had promised an old set of dishes to this year's church bazaar.

"Sure, I remember what happened," she said.

146

"But neither Alverna nor the Candyman told me what was going on. I thought they were just passing sweet notes. I was about ready to go to the Candyman's when the Philosopher came calling. He was going that way, so I gave the letter to him to deliver. I still have the picture in my head. He tucked the envelope inside the magazine he was carrying and strutted off like he owned the world."

Mom wrapped another plate and had it halfway to the packing box when her hands stopped moving.

"Oh, Lord!" she cried. The plate crashed to the floor. "That was the day of the scavenger hunt. It was the last time I ever saw the Philosopher alive. It was the day he died."

We found the marriage proposal and the answer, tucked in the old magazine at the bottom of Dad's scavenger-hunt box.

I started running again, with Deever right behind me.

"Pat, I'm not kidding. You slow down, you hear? There's no need to run anymore. We know all the answers."

But we didn't know the most important answer of all. We didn't know what Miss Alverna and the Candyman would do when they found out what had happened.

Miss Alverna listened while we talked, shaking her head slowly and sadly all the while.

"All those years wasted," she said. Her hands

were in her lap. She folded and unfolded them. "Every time I went to buy candy, I promised myself that I would walk into his store and stare him in the eye. But it's too late. We're different people now."

She wouldn't change her mind, no matter how hard we talked.

When we told the Candyman, his eyes saddened more than before, and his shoulders drooped. The words he spoke then showed the same kind of pain as Miss Alverna's had. When we told him about her weekly visits to buy candy, his face softened, but he just sat there, lost in thought. Finally we left.

"So, what are we going to do now?" I asked. We were walking up the street toward the *Tickfaw Chronicle* office. Deever kicked at a pebble on the sidewalk. Her mind was someplace else. When we got to the office, she found a chair in the corner and sat down, frowning, staring at her fingernails, still not saying a word.

"That child sick?" Dad asked.

"She's thinking," I told him.

"Oh, that what it is? I didn't know thinking was so painful."

Dad went back to his typewriter and a little of the quiet went away. Then suddenly all of it went away.

"Patrick!" She was on her feet, headed my way, a mile-wide grin on her face. "How much money you got?"

When Deever asks that question, it usually means whatever I've got now, I won't have shortly. But she didn't take any money from me. She sent me out doing errands to spend it. When I came back, I had two red roses from Finley's Grocery and a bag full of peppermints from the Candyman.

"Good," she said. "Now, you take the roses and this envelope to the Candyman." She handed the envelope to me. It was a plain white envelope. Nothing special about it. "And I'll take the peppermints and this other envelope to Miss Alverna."

The big smile was still there. She was up to something.

"You going to tell me what you're doing? After all, it's my money we're spending," I said.

"Nothing special, Pat. Anyway, if you know beforehand, you'll probably give it away."

"Deever, I'm not moving one single inch until you tell me."

Her smile dimmed. "I'll tell you part."

"Not part! All of it!"

"The part I'll tell you is that *his* marriage proposal is in her envelope and *her* answer is in his envelope."

That's dumb, I thought. "You need a better idea than that."

"You're right, Pat. And that's the part I don't think I'll tell you."

"You better tell me! And you better tell me now!"

149

She shrugged her shoulders. She didn't mind one bit that I was jumping and shouting. And I knew it.

"Well, Deever, tell me then!"

"I changed the notes a little bit."

"Aw, Deever, Miss Alverna and the Candyman are angry. Those notes tell how they felt twenty years ago. They don't tell how they feel now." But she had gotten me thinking. Did Miss Alverna and the Candyman really feel different?

"You know what I think would work best of all?" I went on.

She smiled like she knew the answer to my question.

"If we could turn back the clock and get him to propose and her to accept, all over again."

She nodded, then nodded some more, like I was a little kid who had finally caught on that two plus two is four.

"So, Deever, you going to tell me how you changed the notes?"

She gave me a wink but didn't say a word. And then suddenly she didn't have to. I knew.

Those notes weren't twenty years old anymore. She had put today's date on them.

The Richest
Person in Town

The first thing Violet Deever decided was that she needed a second job, because she wanted to make more money than she was getting from her job at Mr. Harter's Drug Store.

"I don't know what I want to do with it, Pat," she said, answering my question. "Maybe I just want to have it in case there is something I want to do with it."

The second thing she decided was that, since my dog Ezmerelda had two new pups, we could sell them and make money that way.

"I got mixed feelings about selling those pups, Deever. They're kind of cute. Anyway, who's going to buy a dog? People give dogs away all the time in Tickfaw."

We had just fed Ez and the pups and were sitting on the back steps, watching them fight for the food in the tin pan.

"Suppose we taught them to do tricks? That would make them worth a lot of money."

"Pups aren't worth a darn at learning tricks. Besides, Ez is really my dad's dog, so the pups are probably his, too."

But she wouldn't quit. She insisted that we ask Dad if it would be OK to sell the pups, and he surprised me when he said yes.

We should have made plans for the selling, but we didn't. We started down the block at the Finleys. They've got a big yard, and Mr. Finley runs the grocery store on Main Street, which ought to keep sensible puppies fat and happy.

Mrs. Finley was weeding her garden. Gardening's what keeps *her* happy. She stopped when she saw us.

"Good morning, Pat. How's your father and mother? And who is the lovely little lady you have been spending so much of your time with lately?"

Something smelled funny. It was coming from the bucket at her feet. I checked it and it was full of fish heads. When Mrs. Finley saw me looking, she smiled.

"I'm planting them in my garden," she said. "They smell dreadful, but they are good fertilizer."

I introduced her to Deever. "She is staying at our house for a while," I told Mrs. Finley.

"Where are you from, Violet?" Mrs. Finley asked.

"I've been in Tickfaw since the start of the summer," Deever said, kind of dodging the question. "We were wondering if you would like to buy a puppy that can do tricks. We can go get him and show him to you, if you want us to."

But Mrs. Finley wasn't interested. A dog would just dig up her garden, she said.

"But I know someone who might want another dog," she said. "Ask Fiddle Townlee."

Fiddle was a friend of mine. Also of Deever's. I hadn't thought about selling a puppy to him. And Mrs. Finley had said *another* dog. I didn't even know that he owned one dog, much less that he'd be wanting another.

It was almost time for Deever to head for her job at the drugstore. First we went home for a snack. We would visit Fiddle in the afternoon.

We were snacking when the phone call came for Deever.

She stood there with the phone to her ear, listening, unsmiling, twirling the cord in her fingers.

"I don't think so," she said. "I'm OK right where I am."

It had to be her father. He had left town in a hurry early that summer, one step ahead of the Sheriff. That was when Mom had said Deever could stay with us.

"No," she said into the phone. "I won't change

my mind." There was a pause. "Good-bye." She hung up the phone as gently as if it were made of eggshells.

Then she saw me watching.

"Mind your own business, Patrick O'Leary!" she said sharply. She brushed past me and out the front door. I started to follow, but suddenly there was a hand on my sleeve. Mom had been watching, too.

"She just made a big decision, Pat. Let's let her alone for a while."

I sat still for ten minutes, but I couldn't sit still any longer than that. When I got outside, all she wanted to do was play with Ezmerelda and her puppies.

"Maybe we shouldn't sell both of them," she said. "Maybe we should keep one." She was pointing to the runt of the litter, who was sniffing at a weed.

When Deever headed for her job at the drugstore, I went looking for Mom.

"Mom, you think she's really going to keep staying with us?"

"I don't know, Pat. She's welcome to. For now, anyway. But if her father really wants her to be with him, she may have to leave."

"We've had a pretty good summer, Mom." All the nice things that had happened filled my head. For a second I couldn't think of a single trick Deever had pulled on me. It was almost like she was a saint. I grinned at the thought.

"Yes, we have had a good summer. But we can't

turn it into a tug-of-war, Pat. We should let that child know she's welcome, but we should also let her make up her own mind."

When Deever came home at noon, Mom fixed us leftover chicken sandwiches. I began eating, but Deever just sat there. Mom got up to go after the milk.

"My daddy phoned again this morning at the drugstore," she said suddenly. Mom stopped in her tracks.

"He said if I had enough money for a bus ticket, he would meet me in New Orleans." Her hands were clenched in her lap. She lifted her head and looked at Mom's back. Mom slowly turned. "I almost got enough from what I earn at the drugstore," Deever said.

"Will you go?" asked Mom.

"He seems lonely," Deever answered. "I never had such hard thinking to do." Her voice was so low I almost didn't hear the words.

It was quiet. Too quiet. "Deever, let's go see if Fiddle really does want a puppy," I said.

Fiddle Townlee lives with his brother, Mr. Vernon Townlee, who runs the bank. Dad says they are probably the richest family in town. They live in a big house right in the center of Tickfaw. But once you get inside the front gate, you'd never know you were in the center of town. It's like a park, with grass and oak trees everywhere.

Mrs. Townlee opened the door. She is a tiny,

bubbly lady with silvery hair. Mom says she used to be a high school cheerleader, and I believe it.

"How nice of you to visit Fiddle," she said, with a big smile. We followed her through the house toward the kitchen. Everything sparkled. The floors were shiny hardwood. The dining-room table was large enough to sit two dozen people. A crystal chandelier scattered rainbows of light everywhere. I turned to Deever. Her eyes darted left and right, up and down, never stopping.

"Fiddle's in the backyard, but he'll be in in a moment. Sit down and I'll get you some ice tea," she said.

The kitchen was bigger than our living room. The house was a beauty, all right. But now I was looking out the kitchen window into the yard. It was the size of the Town Square, only prettier, with pecan trees and white camellias in all the right places.

Toward the back, sitting on a white stone bench, was Fiddle. He was staring at something even farther back in the yard. I tried to see what it was, but I couldn't see a thing. Fiddle seemed to be sitting still, doing nothing, staring into space.

In a few minutes Fiddle came in, feet pointed sideways like always. He smiled and nodded when he saw us. He sat at the kitchen table, and Mrs. Townlee brought him a bowl of warm Cream of Wheat. Then she tied a napkin bib on him to keep his front clean. Fiddle stirred in butter and sugar, and then spooned some of it in his mouth. Soon there was a white Cream of Wheat mustache on his upper lip and a small dab of it on his chin. Occasionally he would look at us and smile, but his main attention was on his meal.

We sat at the table in the bright kitchen and sipped our tea.

"I want to live in a house just like this," said Deever. "It's the most beautiful house I ever saw in my whole life."

Mrs. Townlee smiled. She spent a minute cleaning Fiddle up. Then she left us.

The moment she was out of the room, Deever was on her feet. She walked about the kitchen, examining the stove, refrigerator, even the intercom system in the wall. She moved to the dining room, pulled out one of the big chairs, and sat at the head of the table.

"We sure could do a lot of talking at this table," she said. "Wouldn't it be great to live in this beautiful house? Wouldn't it be great to be rich like Fiddle and Mr. and Mrs. Townlee, and have everything you wanted in the whole, wide world?"

"Maybe," I answered. Rich people probably got bored like everybody else. But I was really wondering why Fiddle had been sitting and staring.

"You have everything you could possibly want in the whole wide world, don't you, Fiddle," Deever said.

I got up and walked back to the kitchen window

and stared out, trying hard to see whatever it was
that Fiddle had been looking at. There was nothing
to see.

When I turned back, Fiddle's brow was furrowed. He was still shaking his head, side to side, in
answer to Deever's question.

What was it that Fiddle wanted that he didn't already have? Deever hadn't paid him one bit of attention. She was already jumping around, exploring
all the other rooms on the ground floor. I turned
back to Fiddle.

"All right if I go out in the backyard?"

I walked across the grass toward the stone bench.
I could feel Fiddle's eyes on my back.

The bench was warming up with the day. It was
a beautiful place to sit and watch. I was surrounded
by green grass, cut so even it had to have been
mowed only yesterday. Back toward the house
were the pecan trees and the camillias. In the distance, like a huge fence, were the big oaks, so close
together their leaves mingled. I sat where he had
sat, and looked where he had been looking.

And there it was, a bit of white jutting up from
the green grass, so far away it was almost hidden by
the oaks. I walked toward it. But the feeling was
strong. I was prowling where I had no right to
prowl.

It was a tombstone. Made of some kind of white
stone. A single word was carved on it.

Stella.

I walked back to the house. When I got close, Fiddle moved away from where he had been watching at the window. When I got inside he was sitting at the table. I sat across from him and stared until he looked up.

"Stella?" I asked. "Is that what you want but can't have?"

Fiddle's eyes dropped back to the table. Then he looked up at me and gave a reluctant nod. He wiped his nose on his sleeve. Then he walked slowly out of the room. That was all the talking he planned to do.

Somehow we never did get around to asking Fiddle if he wanted to buy a pup who could do tricks.

Deever worked again in the afternoon at the drugstore. I didn't have a single thing to do. I'd never admit it to Deever, but I wasn't having much fun since she started working. I dragged Ez out from under the porch. The pups followed. We walked to the river and skipped stones. Ez found some shade and sat. The pups chased flies. But they were company.

Deever brought Mom a present from the drugstore. Mom was fixing supper. She wiped her hands on her apron and took the box from Deever.

"Child, you make little enough money at that job without spending some of it on me." Her fingers ripped at the wrapping.

Today it was a pink handkerchief. Yesterday it had been a little glass dog with beady blue eyes. I don't even remember what Deever had given her the day before. It was *my* mom she was giving presents to, and that grated on me a little bit. I don't know why. But it was hard to stay angry long, because Mom really was getting a kick out of those gifts.

"Supper in about ten minutes," Mom said, and Deever and I went out on the front porch and sat.

"I saw you glaring at me," Deever said softly. "But Pat, a person who has his own real, live mother ought to be willing to share her a little bit with a person who doesn't have a real, live mother."

I knew it. It had been dumb to glare. "I'm sorry, Deever."

Everybody was smiling and talking while we ate.

"I started sewing a new dress today," Mom said. Then, with a sideways glance at Deever, she continued, "But I'm not saying who it's for."

"How soon?" asked Deever.

"Pretty soon," said Mom. "How was Mrs. Townlee?"

"Nice, as always," I said.

"But when we got there, Fiddle was sitting in the backyard, perfectly still, just staring," said Deever.

"Guess he's got a right to do whatever he pleases," said Dad.

Deever smiled at him, then dabbed at her mouth with the napkin.

"I like talking at the dinner table," she said.

"Mom, you know anybody named Stella?" I asked.

She thought about it.

"Rich people mustn't have hardly any problems at all," said Deever. Then suddenly she was quiet.

"Nobody named Stella in Tickfaw," Mom said. She picked up the bowl of peas and passed them to Dad.

Nobody expected the next question.

"You think I should go with my daddy?" Deever asked Mom.

Mom didn't answer. She had said to me we ought to let Deever make up her own mind. But now she was having a hard time sticking to what she had said.

"Don't you like it here?" Mom asked, plopping mashed potatoes on her plate. "That dress ought to be finished sometime tomorrow."

Deever smiled at Mom, but the smile faded quickly. She began digging a hole in the middle of her mashed potatoes, so there would be a place for the brown gravy.

We ate but we didn't talk. Nothing got decided that night.

In the morning we agreed to go talk to Fiddle about buying one of the pups. Deever had begun playing with Ez and her pups practically as soon as the sun came up.

"I call this one 'Mr. Curiosity,' " she said, pointing at the runt. "Time they both had names."

"We're going to sell them, Deever. They don't need names."

"Each one's special," she said as she bent to look under the front porch for the one that was missing. She found it and dragged it out.

"Why don't we take this one with us," she said. "Then Fiddle can kind of see what he's buying."

It was Mr. Vernon Townlee who opened the door when we rang the bell. He was a tall, thin man, and quiet. He smiled at the puppy, and then reached out and chucked it under the chin.

"Fiddle's still asleep," he said. "You want to come back later?"

I nodded. "But can I ask you a question?"

"I was just going to take a walk in the backyard," he said. "Walk with me."

We walked. Then we sat like three birds in a row on the very same stone bench where Fiddle had sat. There was still early morning cool in the air.

He pointed toward the oaks.

"You see that?"

He was pointing at the gravestone.

"That's a private cemetery. Only one grave in it. Fiddle says Stella was the finest dog he ever owned."

The puppy was squirming in Deever's arms. She put him down on the grass.

"If he misses his dog so much, why doesn't he get another one?"

"Doesn't want another one. He wants Stella.

Fiddle's a bit confused about that. If he was better at talking, I'm sure he would say that any other dog, no matter how fine a dog, would only be a poor substitute." He stood up and stretched his tall frame. "Time for me to get to the bank," he said.

We were halfway back to the house when the door opened and Fiddle came out and started toward us. The puppy saw him and made a bouncy dash, tongue hanging out and tail wagging. Fiddle saw the little brown ball coming at him and stopped short. He grinned. He reached a hand down, and the pup nipped at his finger. An even bigger smile crept over Fiddle's face, and he looked over at us.

I was looking at Deever. This didn't seem exactly the right time to do any selling. But she went into her sales pitch, anyway. At least, that's what it sounded like at first.

"This is one of the friskiest puppies I have ever seen," she said. Now Fiddle was sitting on the grass, and the puppy was chewing harder on his finger.

Then Deever turned to me. "We've got to hurry if we're going to get there on time." I didn't even know where we were going.

She turned back to Fiddle.

"You think it would be all right if we left the puppy here for about an hour, Fiddle? We are in such a hurry. We'll never make it on time if we have to carry this squirming puppy."

Fiddle was rolling in the grass, giggling. The

puppy was nipping at his ear one minute and slob-
bering all over his cheek the next.

Deever looked over at Mr. Vernon Townlee. He
smiled and nodded. We left.

There wasn't a single word said between us until
we were halfway home.

"We aren't in a hurry to go anywhere, are we?"

She smiled. "Sure we are, Pat. I have to get to
work."

"When do you plan on going back for that
puppy?"

Deever just grinned at me.

That night at supper, she wore her new dress to
the table.

"Help yourself to the spaghetti," Mom said. "I'll
be back in a minute with the meat sauce."

"Could you wait?" said Deever.

Mom turned to her.

"My daddy called again," Deever said. "He's
leaving New Orleans for a business trip up north
somewhere."

Mom sat down in front of her empty plate.

"Will you go?" she asked.

They looked at each other.

"I've got mixed feelings," Deever said.

I wanted to tell her to stay. Summer was almost
over and we could even go to school together. I
looked at Mom to see what she would do. Mom's
eyes were on Deever. It had been like that since she

first came. If Deever left, I was going to get my mom back, full-time. But I was going to lose something, too.

"I've never had a family before," Deever said. "I never sat around a dinner table talking and laughing like we do."

She looked from Mom to me.

"He's my daddy," she said.

After supper Deever and I sat on the front porch, biting into slices of cold, sweet watermelon. Mr. Curiosity was sitting at the bottom of the steps, quiet for a change, watching us.

"Violet?" The name sounded strange. I hadn't called her that since the first day I met her.

She looked at me.

"You want to take Mr. Curiosity with you?"

She dropped her melon and hurried down to scoop up the furry puppy.

"Oh, Pat!" she said. "We could fix a box for him, and I could take him on the bus with me." She hugged the puppy with sticky hands. Then she tilted her head and shrugged her shoulders.

"Daddy's going to give me a bad time about having a dog," she said. "And it won't be like living at the Townlees." Her eyes twinkled at me. "At least, not right away. But once I get him used to the puppy, I'll start looking for a house with a porch for eating watermelon on, and a piano, and a stone bench in the backyard for sitting and thinking."

She stopped talking a minute. She put the puppy down and reached for the melon, giving me a big grin.

"And maybe a chandelier over the big table in the dining room, and roast beef and gravy practically every night, and lots and lots of talking. It'll be just like it is here in Tickfaw."

I listened to her until the dark came. Even when I couldn't see her face anymore, I could still hear her dreams.

RSX 1/98   V58   12/02